Copyright © 2024 by Camilla Harlowe

All rights reserved.

No part of this publication may be reproduced, distributed, or transmitted in any form or by any means, including photocopying, recording, or other electronic or mechanical methods, without the prior written permission of the publisher, except as permitted by copyright law. For permission requests, contact camillaharlowewrites@gmail.com

The story, all names, characters, and incidents portrayed in this production are fictitious. No identification with actual persons, living or deceased, places, buildings, and products is intended or should be inferred.

Book Cover by Camilla Harlowe

SUNLIT SEDUCTIONS

CAMILLA HARLOWE

Chapter One

Chloe

I wake up to a dog giving me very slobbery kisses on the face.

"Morning, Bruiser," I say and start petting him without opening my eyes. Bruiser has been sleeping with me every night for the last three years. I was lucky that I found him when I did. Some bastard left him out in the cold in the middle of the night. In November in upstate New York. I was out for my nightly walk when I found him near the river and could hear him whimpering. I figured he was another victim of one of the backyard breeders. He was small and had a deformed leg. I took him home and nursed him back to health. After some expensive vet bills for the surgery on his leg. Since then, he has gotten extremely well adjusted to the farm and he now helps me run the place.

I get out of bed and Bruiser is quickly at my feet. He is the first to get breakfast every morning. His own rule, of course.

I grab my straw basket and head outside. Bruiser is behind me, he likes to check on all the animals in the morning. I open the chicken coop and toss some food out, and my small army of forty chickens come running outside. It's a good day for eggs, I'll be able to sell them. There's a small shop outside the house. I only open a few hours a day, but I only sell the things I can't eat. It's not really about making money, but about making sure everything gets used.

I collect the eggs for the morning and check the garden. The bell peppers and tomatoes are still doing well even though it's quickly approaching October.

I go over to the dog shelter to give them their breakfast. We have six shelter dogs here, but we have room for twelve. We had a good adoption day a couple of weeks ago, which makes it easier to walk each of them every day. I have a large barn that was converted to a dog shelter. It's not as big as I would like, but they have outdoor time all day. I have lots of cameras to make sure they're safe here at night.

I finish the morning chores and head inside. I cut up the tomato and one of the bell peppers, scramble some of the eggs from this morning, and begin frying it in the pan.

As I sit down with breakfast, my phone beeps.

Good morning, beautiful

I smile at the screen. I wasn't ever supposed to feel this way again.

Morning I text back. I put my phone upside down on the table and silence the ringer. I try not to get too hooked on that thing. Mostly because of the way that Dom makes me feel. It's like I'm standing at the edge of a cliff and someone is pushing me off and I'm clinging to reality. But it also feels like I want to jump and dive into his arms.

I wasn't supposed to fall in love ever again.

I finish breakfast and leave my phone on the table. It's something that I've been practising with my therapist. The idea that I don't need to be constantly checking my messages or checking the security cameras. I am safe and everything is fine.

I get ready and go outside to start walking the dogs. I can take them three at a time, so I'll only need to take two trips today.

It's nice out here by the lake. It's cool but warm enough that I'm comfortable in a hoodie and jeans.

It's taken me a couple of months to feel comfortable leaving the safety of the farm.

There's a large gate and a high-end security system around the farm. It's taken me years to be able to leave without having a friend with me, but once I started taking in the shelter dogs, I had to give them some more space. So we started their daily walks, out the in woods behind my property. I don't see people there very often even though there are walking trails. Occasionally I'll see someone running, but the closest neighbour is at least five miles away and almost everyone around here is a retiree except for me, so they normally don't venture over towards my property.

I can hear the birds chirping and some movement in the woods in the distance.

I haven't used headphones for the past four years, and I don't think I'll be using them at all any more.

I figure the sound is just a fox running as they see the dogs and continue on my path.

Max, one of the two beagles that were surrendered to me a couple of months ago starts barking. He immediately sets off the others. Bear, the other beagle, as well as Rocket, the former racing greyhound. Rocket fixes his eye on something in the distance and lounges toward it, nearly taking me with him.

"Rocket, Rocket stop. You're on your harness," I say, trying to get them to calm down.

The noise in the woods starts to come closer. For a moment I'm worried if it's a coyote.

What I see is much, much worse.

"Chloe," a man's deep voice says from the trees.

"Don't come any closer," I say and pass all of the dog's leashes to my left hand and grab my pepper spray with my right hand.

"I just want to talk," he says.

I immediately recognise this as Justin, my ex-husband.

"You know you're not allowed to be here," I say.

"The restraining order says I can't be within two miles of your house. You've already gone past that," he says.

"It says you can't be within two miles of me," I say, trying to keep my voice from shaking.

"But who is here to say that I'm here?" He asks, smirking.

God, I hate that smirk. I've been seeing that smirk in my nightmares for the past four years.

"Like I said, I just want to talk. Please," he says

"We can't do that and you know it," I say.

"I just want to talk," he says and steps closer. Before I can talk myself out of it, I aim the can at his face and start spraying.

"Bitch!" He shouts, doubling over in pain. The wind carries over some of the spray and I start to cough. I drop the can and start running with the dogs, making it home as quickly as possible.

I look behind me a couple of times to make sure I'm not being followed.

When I finally make it home and within the gates, I drop the dog's leashes and drop to the ground. I gasp for breath. I can still feel the remnants of the pepper spray in my lungs, and I've just run the fastest I've run in my life.

I don't have long, though. He's still out there.

I take my cell phone out of my back pocket and call the police.

"911, where is your emergency?" The phone line operator asks.

"97 Country Road. I have a restraining order against my ex. He's in the woods behind my house," I pant out.

"Thank you, ma'am. And are you in immediate danger now?" She asks.

"I will be. Once he is back on his feet. I know he'll be armed. He wasn't supposed to know where I live," I say. I make it to the back door and go inside, calling the dogs in with me. The others are locked in the shelter still, they'll be fine. But everyone else needs to be inside with me, I can't have anyone outside.

"We are sending officers out there now, they should be there in about five minutes. What is his name?" She asks.

"Justin. Justin Cooper," I say, "please come quickly. He's dangerous," I say and walk over to the sink to pour myself a glass of water to help extinguish the fire in my throat.

"They will be there in about two minutes," she says. Right on time, the police officers show up. I hang up the phone and call my emergency vet.

"Hi, Jas, listen, I need you to come over right now," I say, interrupting her when she tries to say hello and engage in small talk, "I had to pepper spray my ex and I inhaled some of it. I was walking three of the dogs and I don't know if they breathed it in. Can you come over and check them out please," I say.

"Of course. I'll be right there," she says and hangs up.

The police finish their quick walk around the property.

"There's no one here," one of the police officers says.

"I know. He's probably scared off for now. But he won't give up, he'll be back," I say.

"If you have any issues with him call us again. But there's nothing we can do for now," he says.

I say goodbye to the police officers and let Jas in, she comes running up the steps as the police leave.

"What the hell happened?" She asks.

"Justin was here. I was walking three of the dogs and he was in the woods behind the house," I say.

"That bastard, how did he find you?" She asks.

Jas has been a friend of mine since middle school. We met at horse riding lessons and we became fast friends. We both agreed we would go to university together and become veterinarians. Jas hated Justin from the day I met him. He was working at the stables and he was way older than me. He started working there when he was twenty-three, and I was fifteen. Jas was immediately suspicious of him. But I was head over heels for the older guy who loved animals and could get me free riding lessons.

We eloped when I was eighteen. Jas went on to vet school, but I stayed home. Jas and I got into a school in Utah, but Justin never would have let me go that far for school.

So I stayed home and took care of him and took care of the house. I wasn't happy, but I wasn't immediately in danger.

"They'll be ok," Jas says, interrupting my train of thought.

"Are you sure? I breathed in a decent amount fo the pepper spray. It still hurts a little," I say. I'm more concerned about the dog's safety than mine.

"If it was really bad they would be throwing up by now. And if they do give me another call. If there's any blood call me right away.

But let them all sleep in the house for the next couple of days so you can keep an eye on them. And give them lots of clean water, of course," she says.

"Of course. I'll keep a close eye on them. Thank you so much," I say.

"So are you having anyone stay over tonight?" She asks.

"No. No, just me," I say.

"I'll go home and get my bag," she says.

"No, you don't have to," I say. She has a wife and a child, I don't want her to feel like she has to come over and worry about me when she has so much more to worry about.

"You're not staying here by yourself with that dangerous lunatic lurking in the woods. Besides, eventually you'll need to take the dogs outside. And I don't trust that fence, I always wanted you to get a wall," she says.

She's right. I made the fence work because I needed something that could be erected quickly, but a wall would have been better. But I also hate the idea of blocking out the beautiful view of the trees, and blocking the dogs from seeing the birds and squirrels.

But it's possible to climb a fence. Or point a gun through one.

I just can't risk it. I know what he's capable of.

Chapter Two

Dom

I finish up the annual presentation. Aegis has had another fantastic financial year, in no small part because of me, and next year is forecasted to be even better.

Benji hangs around in the boardroom after the meeting like he normally does.

"Another good year," I say.

"Don't worry, you'll get your bonus," he laughs.

"That's not what I mean," I say.

He looks up confused.

"Ok, I also want that," I say.

"Good. I was worried you were sick or something," he says.

"Speaking of being sick," I say, "I think you need a break."

"A break from what?" Benji asks.

I gesture around the boardroom. Sometimes I swear he is the smartest idiot I know.

"No, we're not taking a break from work. There's too much to do," Benji says.

"I just think you're going to get yourself burnt out," I say.

"Not possible," he says.

He says that like he hasn't been working without a day off for the past ten years. He's been working nonstop for years to build the company. In university, he was working to pay his own way. He even worked to help with the bills when he was in high school. If anything he's closer to burn out than he ever has been before.

"Sadly, you don't have a choice," I say.

He raises an eyebrow at that statement.

"Excuse me?" He asks.

"I took the liberty of booking us something," I say and pull a manilla folder out of my briefcase. I open it on the table. Benji looks down, disappointed.

"I'm not going," he says.

"You literally have to," I say.

"I literally don't," he says, closing the folder and sliding it back over to me.

"I've already notified the team you're going to be away next week. It would look weird if you cancelled now. And besides, we've been talking about this for *years*," I say.

Benji knows I have him trapped. The company is still new and the investors are very tuned in to what's going on. They don't want to see him rearranging his vacation plans or they'll think that we're working overtime to help fix a system issue with the new software.

We started this company when we were in our final year in college. Benji likes to take the credit for himself because he's the tech guys behind it all, but Aegis never would have taken off without me. Benji is great and he knows what he's doing with software design, but he never could have developed the pitch deck and gotten the investors on board. Not to mention the marketing, he never could have gotten here without me.

But he does work hard. And I do want him to take a break. And we've been talking about going on a vacation or ages, so I finally took matters into my own hands.

We wanted to go to Indulgence Island in Mexico, specifically. Benji and I both have…diverse interests. Once I got over the idea that it was strange for two friends to go to a swingers resort together, I got excited to go. I didn't think I would feel confident enough going alone. Plus there can be a bit of a stigma with single males going to these lifestyle resorts alone. We're not interested in doing anything together, but it's nice to have a friend who understands the lifestyle.

"When was the last time you texted her?" I ask.

"This isn't about Megan," he says, "I'm done with her, for real."

Sure it isn't. He hasn't gotten over the girlfriend that left him last year. And I haven't settled down once in my life. But I think there's someone on the horizon who might change that. I think he just needs one crazy night - or week - with beautiful women and he'll move on from her.

"Please go with me," I say. Normally I wouldn't beg, I don't want him to think I'm desperate for him to go. Even though I absolutely am.

"Fine," he says after a moment, "I think I could use the vitamin D. But I promise you there will be no one there I would ever be interested in," he says.

"You don't need to find your soulmate," I say, "just have fun. What's the worst that could happen?" I ask.

"I find my soul mate," he says.

"Go home and pack your bags. We leave in a couple of days," I say.

"You're an asshole," he says as he leaves. He can call me what he likes, but I can see his shoulders relax slightly as he leaves. The vacation is working and he hasn't even gone yet.

I pull out my phone and open the dating app.

He's agreed to go, I text.

Good. I can't wait to see you, Chloe texts back immediately.

I went on a swingers lifestyle website a couple months ago and made a profile. I didn't expect it to go anywhere. Maybe I would meet someone locally in the city to have some fun with.

But luckily for me, I met Chloe straight away. She was shy at first, not really opening up. But she said she'd been out of a bad relationship for a couple of years now and was finally ready to get back out there. She said she was always interested in the lifestyle but didn't know where to start. Over the past couple of years, she'd been to Indulgence Island a couple of times. I not so subtly mentioned that I would love another trip myself. It has a good reputation in the lifestyle community, so I'm not surprised we've both been before.

That's when we started arranging a trip together. It's taken months to arrange everything. She has to hire a farm hand to take care of all her animals, and I made sure I was working overtime for the past couple of weeks to make sure that nothing will get missed at the office.

But I know it'll be worth it once we're on the beach together.

I pack up and decide to take the subway back home.

Benji has a car service that will take me home whenever I need it, I just have to call. Which is convenient, especially on long nights at the office before a board meeting presentation is due. But I like taking the subway. I like the anonymity. Benji and I are from a small town in the middle of nowhere. Everyone knows everyone's business there. You walk down the road and you feel like someone is telling their friends about it. You go through a breakup and people you haven't spoken to in years know about it. Not here, though. In New York City you can be anyone you want. No one stands out because everyone is different. You take the subway and there are thousands of people all with their own lives. And nobody cares about me or what I'm doing.

I get on my stop and wait in the sea of people. My next stop isn't far away. The office is in Manhattan, and so is my apartment. I pay way too much for a high rise in the centre of the city.

After an uneventful ride home, I arrive in my cold and empty apartment. I started renting here when Aegis got its first big investors. After hiring the people we needed to start building our first software and getting our first office space, Benji and I both splurged on apartments. When we first moved here we were living together in a small studio apartment. I wanted to die. It was horrible, but we had to pay our dues in the city until the business started making more money. Then we developed facial recognition software and sold it to the New York City police for seven figures. It was rolled out immediately and was used for locating missing people. I slept well that night knowing we were doing something good, and we were being paid handsomely for it.

One thing I didn't expect though is that the expensive modern apartment would feel so cold and empty when I'm here alone.

Which led to a couple of years of cycling through hookups trying to fill the void.

I didn't want to cycle through people, but the women I was meeting on apps were here for a vacation or just passing through. People who needed to find themselves so they went to New York to do it. Eventually, they got priced out of the city, or there was someone missing them back home. Or there was just no connection in the morning.

I developed a bit of a reputation, but I didn't do much to prove to anyone that I was able to hold down a relationship.

Benji moved in with Megan, but that didn't last long. After a couple of months, she moved back to our hometown to pursue a relationship with someone she dated in sophomore year. And he started moping around the office and hasn't really stopped since.

I put a frozen pizza in the oven and take out my phone to call Chloe. This has been our routine for a couple of weeks now.

She picks up after a couple of rings. I'm on FaceTime like I normally am, but her camera is turned off.

"Hey, Dom," she says warmly.

"Are you ok?" I ask before greeting her. She's never had her camera off while I called before so it raises a red flag.

"Yeah, yeah I'm fine," she says, her voice shaking.

"You don't sound fine," I say.

"Just a minute, I'll turn on my camera," she says.

"I mean you don't have to. I love seeing you but if it's a bad time…" I say.

"No, it's ok," she says and turns on the camera. She's beautiful, as always, but she looks different. Her eyes are red from crying, and she has large dark circles under them. Her blonde hair which is normally clean and nicely brushed is a mess. And the background isn't somewhere I recognise. I feel like I know every inch of her house already, after the hours we've spent on FaceTime together over the past couple of months.

"I'm staying at a friend's house," she says after noticing the look of concern on my face.

"Yeah, of course. You don't like you've been sleeping," I say. I don't to offend her but I'm worried.

"Not really. It's just a little bump in the road. I'll be fine," she says.

"Tell me if you need anything, ok?" I say.

"I will. And hey, it's only a week to go until we're together on the beach," she says. The idea of it sends a warm feeling spreading through my chest.

"One week," I say.

One more week until I can hold her in my arms and know she's safe.

Chapter Three

Chloe

Jas looks at me judgementally over a cup of coffee. I'm still at her place, and I probably will be until I leave for my trip. Luckily James, the farmhand I call when I need help, was available a couple of days early so he can take care of the animals now.

"I've been there before," I say.

"Well yeah, but not alone," she says.

I look down at my coffee. She'll be able to read my mind if I'm not careful.

"And I just don't think it's safe," she says.

"Jas. I can't stay in your guest bedroom forever," I say.

"You know you're more than welcome to," she says.

I know I am. I know that if she had her way, I would move in with her and her wife so she wouldn't have to worry about Justin coming back to the farm.

After Justin's arrest a couple of days ago, he was released almost immediately on conditions. I wasn't happy that he was released, but I wasn't surprised either. It's happened before and I'm afraid that it might happen again.

I've still been going over to the farm every day, but Jas insists on coming. I was able to take Brusier to her house with me. James has been so helpful, but I still want to visit the animals as much as I can. Jas didn't want me back on the farm to check up not the place at all, but I don't want to spend too much time away.

I wish I lived somewhere I could just pick up and leave. Somewhere Justin could never find me. But then again, taking care of the animals has been my reason for living over the past months when I didn't think there was much else to live for. At the end of the day, there were animals that needed to be fed, and have vet care, and dog adoption applications that I have to review. We've been having a lot of dogs being adopted recently, but we immediately take in as many as get adopted out.

"I can't stay with you. I need to stay with the animals. It's fine for a week or two to get some help, but they need me. And besides, I can't move in right before I go on vacation," I tell her.

"So you're determined to go, huh?" Jas asks. She's normally happy for me. I've been to Indulgence Island a couple of times in the past. She supports me in the lifestyle, nothing like that would ever keep her from being my friend.

"I just don't want you making any reckless decisions," she says, "I know the breakup with Justin was really hard. And I want you to be happy, I just want to make sure you've dealt with everything," Jas says.

She knows for a fact that I haven't dealt with it.

The relationship with Justin escalated quickly. We met at a lifestyle event and I went home to his place. We fell quickly for each other and he moved in with me at the farm.

When I wasn't working, we spent time taking care of the farm and working from home. Justin had a pretty flexible job, so we were able to take a trip to Indulgence Island within our first month of being together. We had an amazing time and it felt like a dream.

After that, it started to turn dark quickly.

Justin became very controlling. He suddenly got the idea that I was cheating on him. He was going through my phone and when he found nothing, he turned violent.

After it got physical, I called the police first and then Jas second. I stayed with her for weeks until I felt safe to go back home. Since then, he hasn't stopped bothering me. The police know but when he's sending me emails or text messages they can't do much. They come out when he comes to the farm. Luckily that's only happened one other time. But every time it happens it's terrifying.

At least this time I have a reason to flee the country so I can relax. I jut hope Dom is the person he seems he is.

I'm exhausted from losing sleep. I'm terrified Justin will be waiting for me when I go back to the farm to pack my bags. Jas is coming with me though, she wouldn't hear about me going there alone.

I first take a look at all the animals. They're all fine and happy. James has been doing well with the animals, but I've missed them. Jas and I take the dogs out in the woods for a quick walk and some time in the backyard to play.

Once we're done, I pull my suitcase out and get packed up.

"Are you sure you'll be ok?" Jas asks. Her face looks concerned. I open my arms and pull her in close, resting my face on her shoulder.

"Thank you so much for everything," I say.

"You have all the security cameras on?" She asks.

"I do. And we have a house and animal sitter who knows about the situation. He knows to call the police straightaway if there are any issues, and I've checked the fence. There's no problems with it and the alarm is turned on," I say.

Justin has never tried to hurt one of the animals, but I'll make sure he never has the opportunity either.

It was a little strange to explain the situation to my farm hand, that my abusive ex might try to show up. But considering he's released on conditions he should be staying far away from here.

I stayed with Jas that night and she brought me to the airport the next morning.

"Thank you so much for this," I say and pull her in for a hug again," I say.

"Any issues, please call me right away," she says.

I know she's going to worry about me. But I do trust Dom. I think he's a good guy and I need to see if this is going to go anywhere.

I drop my bags and make my way through to security. My first stop is a very strong coffee which I need.

I try to read a light romance novel so I can get myself into a relaxed mood for a vacation. I keep checking the security cameras in the barn, and the animals are fine. Everything is fine. No one besides Jas and Dom knows where I'm going Justin can't get me where I'm going. I only have a three-hour flight until I land in Mexico where I can have unlimited cocktails and Dom can hold me in his arms. I feel like I'm falling apart on the inside and I just need something to help put me back together.

When I land in Mexico the warm air envelops me. I can't wait to get changed into a sundress at the resort. The jeans and hoodie I wore on the flight started to feel claustrophobic.

I take the taxi waiting for me outside the airport which takes me a short ride to the resort.

I'm here I text Dom as I check in at the front desk and get my desk key.

Seriously? He texts back straight away

I can't believe you're actually here he texts again quickly. I'm not sure if I want to go to my room first and get used to the idea of seeing Dom in person, or if I should meet up with him. It seems a little strange that he's here somewhere waiting for me. I wonder if he finally told his friend that he wanted to meet up with me.

Come meet me at the lounge bar when you're ready he texts. I agree to meet him and quickly get ready. I decide on a light blue sundress. It's not too revealing, though I have plenty of sexy outfits for later if we need them, which I hope we do.

I quickly brush my teeth and my hair. My hair is looking flat, so I run my fingers through it to help revive it. It doesn't work. I add another layer of makeup to help conceal the dark circles under my eyes and add some blush. I hope after a day or two in the sun I might be able to catch up on some sleep and get some sun. I look like I could use it.

I'm as satisfied with my appearance as I can be, so I take my cross-body bag and swing it across me. I check I have my phone on loud in case there are any issues with the farm, and I have my room key.

I make my way upstairs to the lounge bar. It's exactly the way I remember it, with a pianist playing jazz music gently. It's late afternoon so the lounge bar isn't busy yet like it is after dinner once people are ready for a glass of wine after their meal. There are a couple of people sitting there with company. There's a set of three people, two women and one man, clearly flirting with each other. A woman is reading a book and sipping on a glass of red wine. There are large windows overlooking the cliffs and the ocean. The furniture is all clean white like the walls. There are small accents of light blue around the room, giving the place a clean and modern feel.

I scan the room, looking for Dom.

"Chloe?" I hear a voice say behind me. I turn around and see him. He's walking back from the bar. He's holding a glass of white wine in each hand which he quickly puts down on the first available table.

I walk over to him as quickly as my high heels will allow me. I can't barely believe he's standing in front of me. He has a warm glow to his skin and his light brown hair is highlighted from the bright sunlight streaming in through the window.

Dom opens his arms and I accept a hug from him. He's taller than I expected, he's taller than me even with heels on. I press my face against his broad chest and inhale his scent, a mix of cologne and sunscreen. I look up at him and lean in for a kiss which he accepts.

"I can't believe you're here," he says.

"I wouldn't miss it," I say.

He gives me a tight hug and I feel like the pieces of me that have been missing for months have finally been put back together.

Chapter Four

Dom

Benji and I finally make it through the long line at security at JFK airport.

"Where should we head first?" He asks.

We look at each other and immediately head to the bar. I order us a round of beers. It's busy despite being eleven AM, but I guess time doesn't count in the airport. I decide that our vacation is starting immediately and I need to get as many beers in as possible before we get on the plane.

I keep checking my phone to see if Chloe has texted me.

"Everything ok?" Benji asks.

"I'm fine," I say.

"What's her name?" He asks.

Damnit. I was trying not to tell him about Chloe. Even though I've known Benji for basically our entire lives, it feels weird telling him that I've met a girl online and arranged this holiday to go meet her.

"I can't believe you roped me into this little adventure of yours," he says, reading my mind.

"Listen…" I say.

"So what's her name?" He asks.

"Chloe," I say.

"So is she your girlfriend? Or is she just going to be a hookup?" He asks.

"She's not my girlfriend. And I don't know if she's going to be anything. We've talked about it and we both agree that we're on this vacation alone. We want to meet up and see if there's the same spark in real life as there is online, but I don't want to put too much pressure on it.

"What's she like?" Benji asks.

"She's great," I say, "she's been in the lifestyle for a couple of years. She got out of a relationship about a year ago. He's not a nice guy. She's talked about it a little but not too much," I say.

"What do you mean?" Benji asks.

"I don't know," I say, finishing my beer and motioning for the bartender to bring us two more, "I know he's showed up at her house a couple of times after the breakup. She's pretty afraid of him, so I trust her that he's an ass. I know he didn't treat her well. So it's an open wound right now I think she booked this trip to escape. And she deserves it, she needs to let loose for a while."

"What does she do for work?" Benji asks.

"She has a small farm and an animal shelter," I say.

Benji raises an eyebrow.

"A small farm?" He asks.

"Yeah. I think it's mostly a hobby farm. I know she loves animals, that's obvious. I think she got a fair settlement in the divorce, especially because of the way he treated her. I know what her ex did and I don't care to know too much about him. So I think she's spending a lot of time recovering," I say.

"How did you meet?" He asks.

"On a lifestyle website," I say.

The truth was, I wasn't looking for a real connection. I just needed someone to go to lifestyle parties in the city with. I found a couple of different women to have a good time with, but there were no connections. Just a fun time

Benji looks over to the departure board and gestures with his beer.

"We need to get going," he says and finishes the pint. I do the same and we wait to board the plane.

We arrive at the resort a couple of hours later. I was tired on the flight but I did manage to get a couple of hours sleep. The lay-flat seats helped. But when we got out of the taxi and arrived at the resort, I felt a new wave of excitement. Chloe is going to be here soon. She sent me her flight information a couple of days ago. I'm here for the night and then she'll be here in a couple of hours.

We have two separate rooms on the same floor. We find our rooms and drop our bags. He still looks like a grump even though he's just arrived in paradise

Benji and I get some drinks by the pool to help pass the time. I keep checking my phone to see if there are any updates from Chloe. I can tell from her fight tracking information that she's landed, but she might not have good enough service to update me on where she is. I just hope she actually got here instead of getting cold feet and just going home.

I get a message from Chloe and jump up from the swim-up bar.

"I need to go," I tell Benji.

"I'll hold down the fort here. You have fun," he says. I run to my room and quickly change into a pair of clean shorts and a shirt. I wish I had some time to get a shower, I know I'll smell like chlorine from the pool and I'm a little tipsy from the beers but the idea of seeing Chloe makes me feel like I'm floating.

I go up to the lounge. She said she was going to her room first, so I ordered each of us a glass of white wine, partially just to calm my nerves.

I end up quickly drinking both of them before going back to the bar and grabbing two more.

As I'm walking back from the bar, I see a woman with medium-length blonde hair facing away from me.

"Chloe?" I ask tentatively.

She turns around and I quickly put down the two glasses of wine. I quickly walk toward her and wrap her in my arms.

"I can't believe you're here," I say, holding her tightly in my arms.

"It's been such a crazy week," Chloe says, "I can't believe I made it."

"Can I offer you a drink?" I ask, gesturing to the table.

"Thank you," she says and sits down and takes a long drink of wine. I sit down next to her. She looks beautiful. She looks just as tired as she was on the phone, but she has more energy now. More like the Chloe I've gotten to know over the past couple of months.

Chloe and I spend the next half hour catching up. It feels like we've known each other forever, but I can tell she feels awkward.

"Is everything ok?" I ask.

"Yeah, everything's fine. I'm just tired," Chloe says.

"Well I don't want to keep you for too long," I say, "do you want to go for a short walk? And then we can retire for the night. The sea air is really healing, I think. I think it might help you sleep," I say.

Chloe nods gently. I stand up and reach for her hand. She reaches out a hand, which is well-manicured with long French tips on her nails. I briefly imagine her scratching her nails down my back. I push the thought from my mind - I need to be respectful even though we have already exchanged some very naughty messages. I can't wait to act one of them out, but I want to go slowly with her.

There's a large spiral staircase with high white walls which leads down to the beach. Chloe's light blue sundress swishes as she walks down the stairs, holding on to the high wall.

We walk out onto the beach just as the sun is setting. There's a warm yellow glow over the ocean and the empty sun loungers.

"Thank you for coming," Chloe says.

"Of course," I say, "I wouldn't have missed it. I would have flown to Michigan to meet you if you didn't."

"Sorry, I've been so dramatic lately. I've really enjoyed getting to know you over the last couple of months. Everything has been so crazy and overwhelming at home. I feel like now that I'm here by the sea and with you, I can finally breathe," she says.

I wrap my arms around Chloe and put my fingers on her chin, pulling her face up to gently kiss her. She sinks into my kiss and she sends a fire in my chest. I need her more than I need air. I gently lick her lips with my tongue to open her mouth.

Chloe pulls away quickly, jolting me back to reality.

"Sorry, I…" I say, not knowing what I did wrong.

"No it's not you, it's me… sorry. Sorry, it's all too much," she says and turns on her heel and goes back toward the hotel.

I want to run after her but I don't want to make her feel more uncomfortable than she already does, so I watch her walk into the sunset away from me, not knowing what I've done wrong.

Chapter Five

Chloe

I sit on my bed, waiting for Jas to answer me. She wanted me to check in with her every day that I'm here.

"Hi!" She says when she answers the FaceTime call.

"How are you? How are the animals?" I ask.

"They are amazing. I checked on them today and James is doing a great job.

Everyone is fine, no issues with the fence or the cameras," she says.

"Thank you so much. I've been checking up on them on the cameras. I'm just glad there's no drama at home," I say.

"Have you heard anything from your lawyer?" Jas asks.

"Not really," I say. I've had a couple of emails from them but just saying that Justin was still out and under house arrest and no movement yet from his ankle monitor, which is helpful.

"So how is Dom?" She asks.

"He's good. I mean, he's a nice guy and everything. I'm glad I was able to come here and meet him, but it just seems... different," I say.

"How so?" She asks.

"I don't know. I felt like there was more of a rush when it was online. I think it was the escapism I needed. And now that I'm here it seems very real," I say.

"Is that what you wanted, though? To have a real relationship with him?" She asks.

"I think so," I say, "I think I'm just nervous. I always said I would stay single forever, just me on my little homestead with the animals. But then Dom was changing everything. And he kissed me on the beach yesterday and I completely fumbled it," I say.

Kissing him was thrilling and made me feel like I was at home. I felt safe and content in his arms. But I swore I wouldn't let myself be vulnerable like that again. Dom was just supposed to be sex, but I couldn't even let my mind reach that point with him.

"What happened yesterday?" Jas asks.

"It was just weird. We were kissing, and it was nice. And I just... I don't know, I started to panic I guess. It was like memories of being with Justin were flooding back to me and I felt like I was suffocating," I say.

"It sounds like you were close to a panic attack," Jas says.

She knows I've had them before. Mostly after Justin attacked me in the past or when we've had other issues with him. Those were much worse. I was able to get myself out of the bad situation but as soon as I was safe, my body shut down completely. It was like I was in a comatose state, but my breathing was heavy like there was someone sitting on my chest. Eventually, I was able to get myself out of that state by reminding my body that I was fine.

Since Justin left, I haven't been with anyone physically.

I'd sent Dom photos of myself when we were long-distance. I enjoyed it, but that was easier because I was in the comfort of my own home. I was safe. Now, I don't know. What if he's dangerous?

I wasn't supposed to let myself fall for him, but it happened anyway. I guess sometimes you can't control these things.

"Are you seeing him at all today?" Jas asks.

"Yeah, I think I have to," I say, "the resort isn't that big, and it would be rude if I actively avoided him," I say.

"I think you should make plans to see him again," Jas says.

"I'm so embraced about yesterday. I don't even know what to tell him," I say.

"Just be honest with him," Jas says, "he knows about Justin, doesn't he?"

"I told hi. I don't know if he fully understands how bad it was, but I don't expect him to," I say.

It's hard to describe to someone. I don't want to sound dramatic. Even though I would never embellish the truth or be untruthful about what happened. But it was a lot, I never wanted him to stop believing me.

"How's the weather there?" Jas asks, breaking up the tension. I know she doesn't want to send me into another panic attack or spoil my mood by talking about Justin.

"Oh it's incredible," I say, "it's almost too hot today. But not quite. When I got off the plane I felt like I could feel all my problems melting away. I guess that didn't last too long. But I do feel like the sun is making me into a brand new person," I say.

"Good. You deserve it. Now go see Dom and talk to him. Smooth over what happened yesterday. I promise he won't be mad at you. Be honest. And let yourself relax. Justin isn't there, he can't hurt you. But you can let him ruin your trip. And you deserve this time to get back to feeling like yourself," she says.

I message Dom and ask if he wants to meet in the lounge bar. He messages back immediately agreeing. A couple of hours later, he's waiting for me with two glasses of champagne.

"Evening," he says when he stands and gives me a quick kiss on the cheek. He's wearing a light blue button shirt and white linen shorts. It's hot, I feel sweat start to collect on my brow.

I sit down next to the open window to help catch the breeze. There isn't much of a breeze, but I'm nervous enough about seeing Dom today, I don't want to sweat more than I am already.

"Have you been hanging out with Amelia much?" Dom asks and takes a large drink of his champagne.

"Yeah, I saw her earlier today. She's so nice, and she came here alone. I'm glad I started talking to her, it's nice to have a girlfriend here," I say.

"Benji is obsessed with her," he says.

"Have they even met?" I laugh.

"No, not at all. He saw her yesterday in the sun lounger when you were talking to her and I think it was love at first sight. Or lust at first sight, at least. I know she's his type, and he's been talking about her nonstop," he says.

"He's the CEO at Aegis, right?" I ask.

"He is. He thinks that makes him better than me, but he would be nowhere near without me," Dom says and puffs out his chest slightly.

"I think by definition that makes him more important than you," I laugh.

"That's what he likes to think. But without my savvy business sense, he never would have gotten the investors to pay any attention to him and he would have gone bust. So really, he owes everything to me," he says.

"I'm glad you're so humble about it," I say.

Dom blushes slightly at my comment.

"Sorry, I didn't mean to come off as bragging. I just love my work. It's nice to be able to take something that is just starting out and make it really take off," he says.

"No, I love that," I say, "I never would have wanted to start a big company. But I like that you have. Especially something that's actually good for society, which is nice," I say.

"Do you want to get out of here and go for a walk?" Dom asks.

"I'd love that. Let's go down to the beach and have a redo of yesterday," I say.

There's a comfortable silence as we walk out of the main lobby and down toward the beach. The sun is still high in the sky and people are out lounging on the beach. I wish it was later, as I feel the sweltering heat surround us.

"I don't think I'll be able to stay out here for long," Dom laughs.

"I don't blame you. It's not as nice as yesterday when it was later. I'm sorry for yesterday, by the way. I didn't expect that to happen," I say.

"Does that happen often?" I ask.

"No, not really," I say, "they're much worse when Justin has done something to scare me. But I haven't… you know, been with a man since Justin left. I think it was just my body not knowing that we're safe this time," I say.

"I promise you're safe with me," Dom says, giving my hand a quick squeeze. His eyes are gentle and concerned. And in that moment, I know what he's saying is true and that I can trust him.

"Would you ever move away from the farm? Would you feel safer that way?" Dom asks.

"No," I say, "I don't think I ever could. I know I don't have a big rescue, but we have enough of a reputation for taking dogs who are scheduled to be put to sleep. I couldn't sleep at night if I knew there wasn't anyone else to take those dogs," I say.

"But you don't feel uncomfortable that Justin knows where you live and he could do something to you?" Dom asks. "I mean, I don't want to scare you again… and I don't think he actually will try anything."

"No, it's ok. I know the reality of it. And it's just a sacrifice I have to be willing to make, I guess," I say. I'm realising that I don't make much sense. If I want to be fully safe, I should be willing to leave the farm. But I'm not, so it's a risk I'll take.

"Would you ever leave the city?" I ask.

Dom takes a moment to think about it.

"I don't know. It would make work for difficult. And as much as I think Benji can be an idiot, he's my idiot and I like seeing him every day. And we work well together so I think that work would suffer a little," he says.

"But do you like living there in that big city?" I ask.

"I think I do. I like the anonymity of it all. But sometimes it would be nice to live somewhere quieter. I guess I'm open to seeing what comes," he says.

There's a moment of silence before Dom leans into me.

"Is this ok?" He asks, putting his hand around my waist.

"Yes. It feels nice," I say and lean in to gently put my lips on his. I take it slowly but it feels fine.

He starts to kiss me more deeply and I feel my heart making somersaults in my chest. I feel safe in his arms, and I never want him to let go.

Chapter Six

Dom

I'm so glad that Chloe opened up to me about what happened yesterday. I really thought it was me, like maybe she didn't like me after meeting me in person, so I was doing something wrong.

I hate that she had a flashback to being with Justin, but I hope I can help her out of it.

After she gently kisses me on the beach, I feel like I could fly over the water.

"I have a bottle of wine in my room. If you want to go back…" I say. I feel like I'm taking a chance by asking her, but it doesn't have to lead to anything. I do want to take her back to my room, but I mostly need to get out of this suffocating heat.

"You know, any place with air conditioning and a cold drink would help right now," Chloe says.

I take her hand and we walk back to the resort.

"Sorry, I am so sweaty," I say, running my hand over my forehead. There's a gross slick across my hand and I can imagine I don't smell very good.

"No, I am too," she says and turns on the air conditioning unit on the window.

"Do you mind if I take a shower and change?" I ask, "I don't want it to be weird, but I don't want you to have to deal with me bring gross for the rest of the afternoon," I say.

"No, it's fine. Seriously. Actually, I might as well, if you don't mind…" Chloe says coyly.

"Yeah, of course you can. Do you want to go first?" I ask.

"No, you go. I have some messages to catch up on. My friend from home is checking up on me," she says and waves her phone in the air.

I nod my head and take a pair of clean athletic shorts out of the dresser and go into the shower. I turn the water on lukewarm. I can't do cold water, but I don't want it to be hot either.

Speaking of hot, it would be incredible if Chloe was in the shower with me...

Damn. Just one moment of thinking about her and I have a problem now.

I quickly shower and get back out so Chloe isn't left waiting.

I don't want to make her uncomfortable so I throw the shorts on instead of walking out in my towel.

I come out and sit down on the small sofa while Chloe takes a shower. She's in there for a long time.

When she comes out, her hair is wet and curling down her back. The small white towel is pinned together in front of her. Her skin glistens with the small water droplets.

"So one thing I thought about in the shower was that I didn't bring any clean clothes with me," Chloe says.

"There's a pair of bath robes in the closet. If you wanted to give me your room key I could also run over there and get you some clothes," I say.

"No it's fine," she says and sits next to me on the couch. I try not to stare at her too awkwardly, but the towel is riding up and exposing her toned inner thigh.

"Thank you for being patient with me," she says, trailing her finger down my arm.

I quickly remember I'm not wearing any boxer shorts, just the navy blue athletic shorts I slipped on after my shower. Not my best decision, as her gentle touch is making my mind wander.

"Sorry about that," I say and glance down at my erection poking out through the bottom of my shorts. I stand up to readjust myself and pull the shorts back down as they'd ridden up.

"No, it's ok," Chloe says and puts her hand on my knee. She leans in and gives me a kiss as her fingers trail up my shorts.

"Are you sure this is fine? Not moving too quickly?" I ask in between kisses.

"Absolutely fine," she says and reaches up my shorts to grab my cock. I moan and lean back as she starts pumping up and down.

"Wait," I say and I get up to shake off the shorts. Chloe unties the towel and lets it drop on the sofa underneath her.

I've seen photos that she sent me when we were long-distance, but she looks even better in person.

She bends over and puts my cock in her mouth. I moan as she bobs up and down. I run my fingers down her tanned back and end at her ass, cupping it in my hand. I give her a gentle squeeze as she continues sucking my dick. She looks up at me and makes eye contact. Her stunning blue eyes look up at me and give me the go-ahead. I give her a small smack on the ass and a small smile crosses her lips.

I focus on her in front of me. Chloe comes up for air at some point, drool coming down from the side of her mouth which she sheepishly wipes away with the back of her hand.

"I want to be inside you," I whisper in her ear.

I motion for her to stand up and I guide her to the bed. I would take her on the couch, but I need more space. I don't want to feel confined the first time I have her.

I continue kissing Chloe as I guide her to the bed. She lays down and I crawl on top of her, running my hand down the length of her body. God, she's perfect. She looks like she was carved from marble, with her large, full bust and round hips. She has light tan lines from laying out in the sun the past couple of days she's been here. I can tell she's fair under the sun-kissed glow she's been developing.

I start at her collarbone and make my way down her body. She opens her legs slightly and I kiss her inner thigh, deeply inhaling her scent.

I can feel her wetness spreading onto her thighs. I decide it's finally time, and I start kissing her and she moans with relief.

She tastes sweet and I feel myself becoming ravenous with wanting her.

She starts to clench her legs and I know she's getting close to climaxing.

I decide I need to finish inside her, so I step away and she looks around frantically for me.

"Don't worry sweetheart, I'll be back to finish the job," I say and go over to the nightstand where I have stashed a box of condoms. I roll one one myself and go back over to her. I put one hand on the bed next to her head and with the other I bend her knee and open her up, giving myself extra space and leverage. She's smaller than me, so she might need it.

I start slowly but she's wet from the waiting and from my mouth on her. I push the tip in and a small exhale escapes my lips. She feels incredible, even better than I expected.

"Please, I need the rest of you," she whimpers. I want to push the rest of myself in, but I resist. I tease her slightly before thrusting myself inside her.

I don't stop and keep the motions going. I reach down for her clit until I feel her muscles start clenching around me. Her back arches as she comes to an orgasm. I can't resist any more and I finish inside her.

I lay next to her and wrap my arms around her as she pushes her ass into my lap.

"Was that ok?" I ask. I might have gotten a little carried away at the end, but I wanted to make sure she was feeling fine.

"That was incredible," she says, "I feel like I can finally let the past go. At least while we're here. After all, I'm safe here and I don't want him to control me any more. I need to get back to being myself," she says.

We lay there for some time until it's finally time to get up and get ready. Chloe puts on the bathrobe and slippers that are hanging in the closet so she can go back to her room for her clean clothes. Luckily her room is only down the hall so she doesn't have to go far.

"Benji and I are going to the lounge for drinks tomorrow night. Would you like to come with us?" I ask.

"Of course," she says, "I'd love that."

"Good. It's a date, then" I smile and I give her a quick kiss before she leaves.

I take out my phone to text Benji.

I hope you didn't make other plans tomorrow. I told Chloe that we're going out to the lounge tomorrow night and I'd like her to come. Never know, you could meet someone, I say.

Sounds like a plan he texts back almost immediately.

He's in a room on the other side of the hotel. We decided not to request rooms next to each other. The hotel here is nice, but the walls are still thin. People here are open to a lot of things and can often be loud. And hearing Benji having sex was the last thing I wanted to do.

I hope Chloe will be up for some of the more open activities. I have something in mind I'd like to try, some things we discussed when we were long-distance. And I know she's been here before, but that was before her last relationship. From what I understand about Justin, it was a whirlwind romance with just a couple of months of dating and then a year of being married before she had to leave for her safety, where she started building the farm.

I hate that she went through that, but I have so much respect for her. She knows who she is and when she wasn't being treated well she knew she had to protect herself.

When I was growing up I had to work to take care of my sisters. I love my Mom, but money was tight, and I became a bit of a workaholic. But as soon as I speak to Chloe I forget about the weight on my shoulders at work and at home.

I still need to take care of my sisters to some degree. It's different now, but I need to take care of them. And being with Chloe makes me forget about all of that.

When she's here, everything melts away and it's just the two of us.

Chapter Seven

Chloe

I get a drink from the bar and lay down on one of the sun loungers. Dom and Benji are in the pool talking to some of the other guests. I occasionally peer at Dom under my large sunhat but I try to be subtle about it.

I hope I didn't weird him out last night. I still really like him, it was just a little too much for one night. Ruby and Dave are going to be here tonight though. I've played with them before, it would be nice to catch up and get acquainted again. It might help me feel more normal. I think I just need some time to get used to being myself again.

I see a woman sit next to me and take out her book. I ignore her for a while while she reads by herself.

After a while, no one has come and said anything to her. I wonder if she is here by herself like I am. That's not uncommon, I've done it myself. I decide to go out on a limb and introduce myself to her.

"Hey," I say, getting her attention. She looks up at me with a smile.

"I haven't seen you around yet, have you just arrived?" I ask.

"Yeah just this morning," she says.

"Welcome!" I say, "are you here with friends or a boyfriend?"

"No, I'm here alone, Just thought I would go out on a limb and book the trip," she says.

"Have you been here before?" I ask.

"No, it's my first time," she says.

"I'm Chloe, by the way," I say and stretch out my hand.

"Amelia," she says and shakes my hand.

We get to know each other. I run her through the resort and its features, like the pain and pleasure room, which is good for heavy and light BDSM as well as voyeurism and exhibitionism. She's interested in Benji, and I don't blame her. He's not my type but I'll admit he is good-looking.

"We're going out to the hotel bar for a couple of drinks this evening. Dom and Benji should be there. Do you want to come?" I ask.

"I would love to," she says.

Perfect. Amelia seems genuine and nice, and I would really like to have a girlfriend on this trip. I hope she does come out with us.

"So if you change your mind and don't want to come out with us, let me know. I don't want to be annoying. But do you maybe want to have a drink together before?" I ask.

"I would love that," she says, "to be honest, I was afraid I'd spend the whole week in my room. This is my first night here and I'm alone, so I'm just grateful for the invitation."

"Amazing. Meet me at the cave bar. We'll get ready and then meet there," I say.

"Ok. Perfect. I love it," she says and smiles, picking up her book. Even under her sunglasses, I can see the corners of her eyes crinkling under the glasses.

I wave at her before I leave. I can tell she kind of wants to get back to her book, but also she's glad for the invitation out with me.

I decide to get a drink before doing a lap around the pool to see if there's anyone I recognise. I wait in the short line and I see my old friend's face light up when he sees me.

"Chloe, love! You should have sent me a message to tell me you are here," Alejandro says. He and I became friends on my first trip here. He's been working here for years, he's the best bartender on the property. And if I remember correctly, he's also one of the smoothest with the women. He and I never hooked up, but I'd be lying if I said I've never thought about it.

"It was a last minute trip. And technically I'm here with a friend," I say.

"Finally a new boyfriend to replace that horrible husband?" He asks.

It wasn't a secret what happened with Justin, but it's still jarring when people ask me about it directly.

"Finally got rid of him," I confirm.

"How are you really?" He asks, pouring extra white rum into my strawberry daiquiri.

"Really, I'm fine," I say, "it was hard at first. And you know what he was like, always acting crazy. But anyway, it's over now."

I don't tell him about Justin showing up at the farm. Jas and Dom are the only people who really know about all that. It just seems too dramatic to talk to many people about. I know they would believe me, but I don't want everyone to worry.

There's a line forming behind me, so I say goodbye to Alejandro and let him work.

"Hey, there's a masquerade night on Saturday, don't forget!" He reminds me.

Good to know. And who knows, I might see him there. It's against the terms of his contract to go to social events with the guests, but he has never been known to follow the rules.

Dom and Benji are in the pool talking to Leanne and Amanda, but I think they're just friends. They're both beautiful, but I don't think either of them are Dom's type.

To be honest, I don't think he has eyes for anyone much besides me. It might sound a little cocky, but it is what it is. I've tempted him for long enough online, I don't think he's going to stray very far.

I think back to when we first met online. It was a website for people in the lifestyle. I had no hits for anyone close to me, so I changed my search parameters to 'anywhere in America'.

His profile was one of the first that came up.

DreamyDom - it was kind of a cringey screen name, but aren't they all? Mine was FarmGirl13, which also wasn't great.

But his picture was what drew me in. He was in the park with a golden retriever, which I later learned was his sister's. He has two sisters. One of them is married and has two children and a dog, and a modest home in New Jersey. The other has been interning with Aegis over her summer breaks for the past two years of university, though she has never really been a good employee. Dom feels like he has to help support her.

Once I scrolled through that picture to the other ones, I realised quickly he was a high flyer in the city. There were pictures of him on the beach, conveniently cropping out another person. One of him and Benji in business class on a flight. I learned later that was to visit their future office in Chicago. And there was one of him and his family sitting around the Christmas tree.

That one was odd compared to the others. The others showed his fancy lifestyle, in his large apartment in the city and with expensive trips around the country. But in the picture of him with his family the house was humbled. It was a small living room, they were all crammed together in front of the short tree. The tree ornaments I could see were clearly handmade by children, and the gifts were wrapped messily, obviously by them and not a professional. I assumed that once one member of the family was Richard successful, the rest would benefit from it. But it didn't look like he was withholding anything. They were all happy, him and his Mom, his two sisters, and his little nephew.

I asked him about that photo one time. After we'd been talking for a few weeks and I'd done my own research into Aegis and how successful it was, I asked if that was an old picture or a new one.

He caught on to it and told me that it was his mother's house. He offered to help her buy a new one but she refused. She said that it was fine when she was raising three children alone, so now that they've moved out she has more space than what she really needs. So she decided to stay at home and Dom and his sisters still had space to visit when they went home, though it wasn't a lot.

When we met, I wasn't expecting it to go far with Dom. I thought that maybe the rich guy would fly me out to New York and we'd have a couple of fun nights at a lifestyle club. But before I knew it, I was opening up to him about Justin. He was telling me all about how he grew up in poverty with his Mom never there as she was working as a nurse on the day shift and then doing an evening shift at a fast food restaurant, only getting a couple of hours in between. So he was taking care of his siblings while she was trying to make ends meet.

I know he did something he wasn't proud of to help bring in some money when he was a teenager.

I decide to stop daydreaming about Dom, and get ready. I decide on a silver backless dress. It hits me at my mid-thigh and tightly hugs my curves. There's a silver chain running down my back attached to a halter top. The back of the dress droops down to the top of my ass, showing off the muscles I've developed from working on the farm. I put on a pair of matching silver heels and do my makeup of a smokey eye and a light pink lip. I was tempted to do red, but I was hoping that I would get some attention from Dom, and I didn't want to deter him from making a move. I decide it's time to go so I head out to meet Amelia.

I get to the cave bar and greet Alejandro. They work hard here, I'll often see the staff working long hours and covering multiple areas of the hotel. It's normal for him to do shifts at the pool bar, do some entertainment, serve some dinner, and then in the cave bar or in the lounge bar until the early hours of the morning. After some small chat, I get two glasses of champagne and put them on the table in front of me.

A couple of minutes later, I see Amelia come out of the resort and toward the bar. She looks incredible, in a form-fitting black dress. She looks like she's slightly uncomfortable. I hope that a glass or two of bubbly will help up her confidence.

"Thanks for coming," I say and Amelia smiles. I give her a quick hug and motion to the drink on the table. We each take a long drink from the flute. The air is warm but there's a slight breeze.

"This is incredible," Amelia says taking in the scenery.

"Isn't it nice?" I say. There are a number of couples around the bar, but it's quiet. There's a young couple playing cards, and a trio flirting with each other.

"Isn't it great?" I say, looking out over the ocean.

We spend the next half hour getting to know each other and having a couple of glasses of champagne.

"So are you ready to go?" I ask, "I need to make sure you and Benji get together. I am obsessed with the idea of you two."

"You said he's rich and owns a company… I'm just a student, he'll think I'm after his money," Amelia says.

"Oh, he is obsessed with you. Believe me. I think he is going to be after you," I say.

"I hope so. Wouldn't it be great if you ended up with Dom as well? He is so hot," Amelia says.

"You can say that again," I laugh.

Chapter Eight

Dom

I'm still trying to wrap my mind around the activities of last night. After we finished the session, Chloe came back to my room and we had a little more fun. But she was tired and fell asleep early. She went back to her room early in the morning for a shower and to get some more sleep, so I met up with Benji for coffee.

I was glad that Chloe actually seemed fine with my voyeurism. She knew I have particular interests, and she does as well, which is why she's been here before. But I wasn't sure if she would have a different opinion on it when it came down to actually doing it. But she seemed just as satisfied as I was at the end of the night.

"So did you and Chloe hook up last night?" Benji asks. We decide to meet over a coffee. In part to debrief about last night, and in part because we both woke up with a massive hangover. I could tell I had too many drinks that were loaded with sugar as I woke up with a raging headache. The only thing I can handle this morning is

"Maybe," I say, "I don't think you need all the details."

"I need at least some of them," he says.

"Yes we hooked up," I say.

"Nice," he says.

"So you and Amelia…" I say, trying to get more information.

"I like her," he says, "but I have a feeling that she's holding back. I don't know. She seemed in to Ruby and Dave, so maybe she would be in to something like that. I mean she wouldn't have come here if she wasn't, right? There's no other reason for her to be here unless to meet someone," I say.

"I know, I just have the feeling she's holding back," Benji says.

"Do you think she's just not used other the lifestyle?" I ask.

"Maybe. I think that might be part of it. But I don't know, I think there might be more going on with her," he says.

"Do you want to figure out what it is?" I ask.

"Yeah, I do. I just feel this magnetism toward her, you know? She was talking to someone else earlier, though. I'm not sure if she wants anything serious," he says.

"I think she does. Chloe said she's crazy about you," I say.

"Yeah, but you know what people are like, especially here. They fall in love at the pool but they've forgotten about you by dinner time. She could have changed her mind already," he says.

"She's going out with us tonight," I say.

"What?" He perks up.

"She's coming out to the lounge with us. I thought I told you. Chloe ran it by her... anyway, she'll be there. It'll be your chance to impress her," I say.

"I don't need to try to impress her," he says, "I own a tech company."

"*We* own a tech company. And I don't know man, she might not really care abut that stuff. Chloe was talking about her and she doesn't seem like she really cares about the money. Nether of them do, actually," I say.

It's one of the things that always attracted me to Chloe. Ever since I met her I imagined helping all her dreams come true. I want to help support her so she can take in more animals, and maybe her some people to help with their care. I don't think she cares if I'm a billionaire or just making enough to live. As long as we're safe and she can help as many of the animals as possible, she would be happy for it.

And I love her so much for it.

I would do anything to make it happen for her.

I spend the rest of the afternoon working. I chose to do it at the pool bar. There's a small indoor area with seating next to large windows so the warm sunlight beams in. I didn't pick the best week to go on a vacation, as there are some projects happening. I've managed to delegate most of my work but I still need to oversee some of the marketing campaigns.

I spend the next couple of hours making up for being gone for a couple of days. I make a mental note that Benji and I need to hire a third in command. The teams are good at what they do, but there's no communication between each other, so things aren't happening while we're gone. I do what to help run the company for the rest of my career, I can't imagine doing anything else. But at some point I need to think about what I want for the rest of my life. Do I want to be in the city forever?

I could manage it for sure. I make good money, which is important if you want to be living in central New York City.

But it's strange to get used to the city. I feel like I'd rather be near my family, mostly to keep an eye on them, even though they don't need me as much as they used to.

"Hey, handsome," I hear from a gentle voice above me.

"Hey, Chloe," I say. I didn't need to look up to know it was her.

"Don't tell me you're working," she says.

"I'm afraid I have to. There's some loose ends I need to tie up or they'll burn the company down," I say.

"Do you need a coffee? Or a snack?" Chloe asks and puts her cocktail down on the table next to my laptop.

"You know, I wouldn't mind one of those. Or both," I say.

She nods and walks up to the snack bar, and a minute later brings over a cappuccino and a large basket of fries.

"Amazing, thank you," I say and take a handful of fries.

"There is really nothing better," she says and does the same.

"So what are you working on? Anything you can tell me about?" She asks.

"Mostly checking in on my little sister," I say.

"She works with you?" Chloe asks between mouthfuls of fries.

"Yes, I made she she had an internship with us. She's family, I had to help her out," I say.

"What does she study?" She asks.

"Computer engineering. She's so smart, but her grades aren't really the best," I laugh, "but she'll be fine."

"What are the rest of your family? What are they like?" Chloe asks.

"They're hard workers. Mom raised us herself, I think I've mentioned that before," I say.

"And you helped her raise your sisters, right?" Chloe asks.

"I did. I looked after them a lot. Not that well, but I'd help them with their homework when Mom was on her evening shift and I'd make us all a simple dinner," I say.

"It must have been crazy when Aegis took off financial," Chloe says.

It's odd to hear her reference it. Of course I know she knows we're successful. It's hard to deny it. But finances have never been at the front of her mind, so I didn't think she ever really considered it.

"It was strange for sure. Especially because Benji and I grew up in the same town, so everyone knew we both owned the company, so it was the talk of the town for a while," I say.

"What was it like?" She asks.

"It was pretty intense for a while. We didn't grow up in a very well off area, so there were a lot of people that asked for a lot of help. We did what we could, but Benji and I didn't give ourselves high salaries for the first couple of years, we reinvested everything. And for what I did make, a lot of it went back in to the family," I say.

"Like what?" Chloe asks.

"Well, when Aegis took off and I felt like the business might survive the first year, one of the first things I did was pay off Mom's house. I wanted to buy her a bigger place, but she refused to let me. She wanted to stay in the place she'd worked hard for for all those years. And if it was good enough to raise three children by herself, then it was good enough for her alone," I say.

"That's so kind of you," Chloe says.

"It was the least I could do after all she did for the three of us. I didn't want anyone getting any ideas and trying to break in and steal from her, though. I made sure she had a good security system and a safer car. She knows her neighbours well and likes them, but I needed to make sure she was safe," I say.

"What about your sisters?" She asks, "Sorry, I don't mean to pry. It's just really interesting."

"No, it's fine, nothing's a secret, " I say. My middle sister, Stephanie, has been doing well since I moved out and started Aegis. Stephanie got married to her high school sweetheart when she graduated from university at eighteen. I was sceptical about the situation, but her husband got a trade and they live a humble but happy life. I do give them generous gifts which ensures they have some more money for a family vacation every year, but her husband supports them, and she's an amazing Mom. She also knows I have money set away for my little niece and nephew in trust, so she knows they're taken care of. Then there's just our youngest sister, Caroline. She partied her way through her first two years of university, nearly failing out until Mom and I had a firm talk with her. She's smart, but she gets distracted," I say.

"How is she doing now?" Chloe asks.

"I told her I would revoke her internship at Aegis if she didn't get her act together. I think she expected to have secured a job even if she just scraped by in school, and I assured her that was not the case. That I knew she was capable of doing well, and unless she put in the effort, it wasn't going to happen," I say.

"And how has she been doing now?" Chloe asks.

"Not amazing well," I laugh, "sometimes I need to call her three times before she picks up during work hours. Seems like she might be away from her desk a lot. But she's getting the work done, and it's done well, so I can't say much to her," I say.

"Maybe she needs some more work or a more complex case," Chloe says.

"Yeah, maybe. I guess I was trying to go easy on her, but I really shouldn't," I say.

"So is that why you're working on vacation?" Chloe asks, "to babysit your sister?"

"Well… a little bit, yeah," I say.

"Give her a bigger project and turn off your laptop. She might call you for help, but ignore her. She'll be forced to problem solve, and you never know, it could help her get more stuck in the work. She's related to you, after all. She's going to want a challenge," she says.

I think she might be right. Maybe she is more like me than I thought.

Chapter Nine

Chloe

Amelia and I get ready in our rooms and I go over to her room just before going to the bar.

"You look amazing," I say and Amelia does a little twirl. She's wearing a black dress that fits her figure perfectly. I decided on a backless silver mini-dress. There's a silver rhinestone chain trailing down my spine.

Amelia and I walk into the club. Unlike the lounge bar, this one is all dark with some red accents. There's red mood lighting which provides just enough to see where we're going, but the room is dark which gives an air of anonymity to everyone in the room. They sometimes have masquerade parties here which allows full anonymity. I make a mental note to check the schedule and see if there are any planned for this week.

Dom and Benji are at the bar. I glance toward Dom, still feeling slightly awkward about my breakdown on the beach the other day, but I appreciate him being so gentle with me.

But I've had time to consider it, and I don't want Justin to control me any more. I'm going to get back to feeling like myself.

"He's so cute," I say to Amelia as she glances toward Benji.

"He's gorgeous. He would never go for me," she says.

"Are you joking?" I laugh, "you're an absolute knockout, especially in that dress.

"He's rich," she says.

"And? All the better to take care of you with."

"Do you know him well?" She asks.

"No," I say, "I know Dom decently well. I've heard about Benji. He's a nice guy. You should give him a chance. And he was asking about you earlier," I say as we make our way across the room.

"Seriously?" She asks. I can see she's trying to hide the excitement.

"Of course," I say, "Dom said you're completely his type. Anyway, I think you should go for it," I say.

I see two familiar faces next to the bar.

"Dave! Ruby!" I say and give them each a hug and a quick kiss on each cheek.

"You look amazing," Ruby says, looking me up and down. I do a cute little curtsey, asking sheepishly.

"Seriously, just as good as I remember," Dave says.

"Oh stop it, you're too kind," I say.

"These are my friends," I introduce Amelia to Dave and Ruby, "we met on a vacation, actually. When I was in London with my ex, we went to a lifestyle party. Well, they happened to own the club," I say.

"Wow, you must be really involved in the lifestyle," Amelia says.

"You could say that," Ruby says seductively, "we've been in it for years. Since we were in our twenties. Anyway, we have a lot of fun. Especially with Chloe."

"So you've…" Amelia says, gesturing towards us. Ruby and I laugh and nod.

"Oh, wow," she says.

Amelia is way too innocent. She is adorable but I feel like I'm going to corrupt her.

After a couple of cocktails and chatting with old friends, I start to feel more myself than I did before. I start glancing toward Dom at the bar. I can tell he's been checking me out and hasn't taken his eyes off me since I got here.

I try to play it cool and wait for him. It works, and Dom starts to make his way over.

"Hey," he says, putting his hand around my waist.

"Hi," I say, turning toward him. Amelia takes this as her cue and slips away to find Benji.

"Sorry about the other night," I say.

"What do you have to apologise for?" Dom asks.

"I just… took off without saying goodbye," I say, "I didn't mean to make it weird. I just started to get overwhelmed again and I felt like I should be in my own room," I say.

"It's fine," he says, "you don't have to do anything you don't want to do."

I lean in and give him and deep kiss. While I do, I feel a similar hand brushing across my shoulders and on my neck. It's not Dom, it's Ruby's slender arm reaching across for me. I turn around and she's facing me, quickly but gently kissing me. I lick her lips slightly and she gently bites my bottom lip. There's a cheer which I only assume came from Dave and Dom.

"Do you want to get out of here?" Ruby whispers in my ear, sending chills down my spine, "You can bring your friend, too."

I nod and take Dom's hand and lead him out of the bar.

After all those months of talking online about what he wants, he's finally going to see it. And I can't wait to show off for him.

Dom and Ruby lead us upstairs to their suite. They have one of the VIP suites on the highest floor. There's a bedroom and a separate lounge room, which connects to the balcony with a beautiful view of the ocean, and a private whirlpool. It's a nice mix of private from the high walls separating them from the balcony next to them, as well as public, as there's a chance that people on the beach below could just see or hear you. From my experience with them, they would be into that. They are attractive, Dave with his well-chiselled abs and muscular back. Ruby has long red hair, which I have pulled on more than one occasion.

Ruby wastes no time by kissing me as soon as we enter the room.

Dom sits in a chair in the corner of the room while Dave makes himself comfortable on the bed. There's a large mirror on the wall so we can all see what everyone is doing.

Ruby hikes my skirt up and runs her fingers along my inner thigh. I feel myself start to relax under her familiar touch. She and I aren't close, but I know she's safe and caring.

She reaches behind me and unzips my dress which falls to the floor. She pulls her leather skirt down, leaving her in just a black thong and her red crop top. She sits me down on the bed and starts straddling me.

Dave moves closer to us and Ruby alternates between kissing me and kissing Dave, all while not taking her hand away from between my legs.

Dom sits on the chair, not saying or doing much.

"Are you ok?" I ask him quietly. His eyes are filled with dust and he gently bites his bottom lip.

"Perfect," he says, stroking himself on the outside of his jeans.

He seems to be fine, so I leave him to enjoy himself while I focus on Ruby.

I reach behind her and undo the tie behind her top, and she pulls it over her head I take her breast in my mouth and start gently sucking on it. Ruby throws her head back and moans gently.

"You were always so good at that," she laughs.

After a moment, Ruby lays me down and Dave moves out of the way. He's taken off his jeans and he's rubbing his large and erect cock.

Ruby starts licking me, I can feel my wetness seeping down my leg which she starts lapping up.

Dave moves around to the back of her and bends her over, entering her from behind. She starts moaning into my pussy as he trusts into her.

I took over to Dom who had unzipped his jeans and taken himself out of his jeans. He's gently stroking himself and looking at me like I'm the sexiest sight he's ever had.

At that moment, I realise why he's really here.

He's a voyeur and this is like his Super Bowl.

I enjoy myself as Ruby brings me to a climax. While she does, I decide to put on a bit of a show for Dom. I arch my back and moan loudly, throwing my legs open so he gets a good view of me.

As I finish, Dave pulls Ruby's hair and pounds harder into her, filling her up.

"That was incredible," she says, lying next to me on the bed.

"I'm not done yet," I say, glancing at Dom who is still stroking himself. He hasn't come yet but he looks like he could at any moment, like he's trying not to because he's enjoying it too much.

I lean over to put Ruby's breast in my mouth again and I put my fingers inside her wet pussy ad Dave's cum drips down my fingers. I continue fingering her until I bring her to climax.

By the time I have finished, I look over and Dom is cleaning himself up. He looks very satisfied with what he's seen.

Dave and Ruby each kiss me before they leave.

"How was that?" I ask Dom as he looks over at me.

"You are incredible," he says and gets up. His cock is already standing at attention again.

"That was quick. I didn't think men can normally do that again so quickly after finishing," I say.

"I can go pretty far. I don't always deny myself satisfaction. Sometimes it's fun, but I can always go around for a second time," he says and lays down on the bed. I crawl on top of him and straddle him.

"Sorry, I haven't showered yet. I might still have traces of Dave's cum dripping out of me," I say.

"Just the way I like it," he says and slips inside of me easily.

"You don't want to taste me?" I ask.

"Come here," he says and gestures for me to come toward him. I don't want him outside of me but I obey.

I sit on his face and he starts feasting on me. I feel myself start to come and he starts licking me harder. Just before reaching climax I get of this face and sit on his erection. He thrusts in to me and before long we both cum. I lay next to him, completely spent.

"That was incredible," he laughs.

"You weren't joking about the voyeurism," I say.

"No, absolutely not. And you looked incredible. But I couldn't let him have all the fun by himself, so I had to join in," he says, wrapping his arms around me and giving me a gentle kiss on the neck.

Chapter Ten

Dom

Chloe and I have a date today. She agreed to meet me after lunch, which gave me some time to work in the morning.

Caroline was actually at work on time today, at least according to Marco, mine and Benji's assistant.

I didn't give him strict instructions to keep an eye on her, but he knows what she's like, so he's normally supervising her when I'm not around.

I review some of the work she's been doing over the past couple of weeks. I don't know how she's managed it, but the coding she's been working on is good. She's been doing it within her team, so I want to say that her team have been pulling her weight, but I know that isn't true. She's a damn smart kid and a great coder, even if she can't show up on time.

After I finish my work, I get ready. I put on a pair of navy blue athletic shorts and a white T-shirt.

I meet Chloe in the lobby of the hotel. She's wearing a crochet bikini top and a pair of denim shorts.

"I didn't know what to wear," she says as she catches me checking her out, "you could have given me some more direction. Surprised dates are difficult," she laughs.

"You look perfect," I say and give her a quick kiss, "should we get going?"

Chloe agrees and I take her hand. We leave through the front door of the resort and walk along the path through the town. There are small cruise ships coming in on the ocean and smaller catamarans with music pumping through large speakers.

"That looks like fun," Chloe says.

"Looks like something I would have done in university," I say.

"You don't strike me as someone who would have been a big partier. Weren't you working a lot?" She asks.

"I work hard and play hard. I have, and probably always will. I didn't have any downtime in school, I was either studying, or in the very early stages of developing Aegis, or trying to drink as much beer as possible in one night," I say.

"I wish I went to university, it sounds like fun," Chloe says.

"Is there a reason you didn't?" I ask.

"I didn't really feel the need. I got an office job pretty quickly out of high school, just a receptionist at a doctor's office. And I was comfortable there. Eventually, I met my ex, and I told him about the dreams I had about starting the farm. He was supportive at the time, but in retrospect, I think it was mostly so he would have more control over me. I was isolated on our property pretty much all the time. We downgraded at the time so we didn't have to spend so much. So we sold my car, we just had his truck which he took in the daytime. I didn't have a vehicle and we were too far away to walk anywhere. I didn't realise he was trapping me until I wanted to leave and didn't have a way."

"What did you do?" I ask.

"I called Jas. I don't have a lot of family, which he used to his advantage. He didn't like me having friends but I always stayed in touch with Jas. We weren't as close and we drifted apart a little while I was with him. But I knew if I called for help she would have been there for me."

"You're lucky to have such a good friend."

"She really is the best. I would do anything for her as well, but it's good to know I have her when I need her. And leaving was so hard, I don't know how I could have done it without her," Chloe says.

I don't want to interrupt our conversation but we've reached our destination.

I looked online for things to do in the area and found an animal sanctuary. There were dozens of types of animals, all ones that were rescued from living in captivity in bad situations. There were types of monkeys and birds, mostly.

I pay our way in, not really knowing what to expect.

"This is incredible," Chloe says, looking at the enclosure. There's a small write-up of each animal and how they got here.

There were birds that were used in travelling shows that have since been shut down. Their wings were clipped in the early days of the shows so they never would have made it in the wild. And monkeys that were used for tourists to take photos with them, but once they stopped making money they were no longer wanted. The rescue took them in to help raise awareness of what not to do while travelling.

We spend the afternoon reading their stories and about the different types of animals. Chloe's eyes light up when a monkey comes up to the window to greet her.

"I feel awful they're still in a cage," I say.

"The lesser of two evils," she says, "at least now they can greet people by choice. I think they're forced to when they're taking pictures with tourists," she says.

We finish in town and get tacos and margaritas from a food truck outside the sanctuary.

"These are incredible," Chloe says, taking a large bite of her taco.

"I think I could eat about a hundred of these," I say.

"Thank you so much for taking me out. I didn't really consider having the resort, but this was nice," she says.

"Do you still want to spend some time outside and enjoy the weather?" I ask, "Maybe we can take a walk along the beach."

"I would love that," she smiles coyly.

We finish and make our way back to the resort property of Indulgence Island. I plan on bringing us somewhere more private. I've been thinking about having Chloe on the beach, and I think today is the time.

I pull Chloe close to me and kiss her on the neck. She throws her head back and inhales deeply.

"We can't…" she says softly.

"And why not?" I ask.

"Resort rules," she says, "we can't play in public in the daylight."

She's right. We'll get a warning if we get caught. And if it happens a second time, we'd get sent home. I rack my brain with an idea of where we can go without getting caught.

Sure, we could go back to my room, but there's no fun in that.

Well, there would be a lot of fun in that, but I'm looking for slightly more.

I take her by the hand and pull her around the side of the hotel. We cross the small beach area and over to the rocks on the other side. I don't think it's owned by any other hotel, and it's harder to get to so I don't think anyone else would see us here.

I climb a couple of the rocks and outstretch my hand.

"I'm going to fall to my death. I'm wearing sandals," Chloe says as she takes my hand and tentatively steps up on the first large rock.

"I promise I won't let you go," I say and give her hand a squeeze and help pull her up as she steps up onto the first rock.

"We should have gone back to the hotel," she says as she lets me carefully guide her up the rest of the way.

I'm taking a bit of a chance, as I've never been up here before. But we're far enough from the hotel that the people on the sun loungers have disappeared, and while there is a public beach ahead of us, it's far enough away we would be able to see a boat coming in and make ourselves more presentable.

I help Chloe up on the last rock and she stands out toward the ocean and takes in the view.

"Wow, it's beautiful up here," she says, "how did you know this was here?"

"I was just checking it out the other day and thought it looked nice. I looked around online and it seems like an area that's not owned by any resort, so we're allowed up here if we wish. And I saw the beach and I knew the view would be just incredible," I say, "but never as beautiful as you."

I start walking down toward the beach and reach out to take Chloe's hand so she'll follow me. My plan to stay up here won't work it's too rocky. I need her on the warm sand.

We finally reach a good area and I pull her in close to me.

My kiss starts gently as my hand reaches the small of her back and I run my fingertips up and down her spine. She's wearing a crocheted bikini top and a pair of white denim shorts.

I imagine her working with the animals at home. She looks beautiful when she's dressed well for an event, but I think she looks best when she's casual and her hair is slightly wavy and tangled from the humidity like it is now.

Chloe starts taking off my shirt, like she's hungry for me.

I reach behind her and pull on the straps of her top, freeing her breasts from the cups.

I pull Chloe's hand down so she sits down on the sand with me. She keeps unbuttoning my shirt as she lays down in the sand.

I feel a flush of excitement as I lay her on her back and she sinks into the warm sand. I trace my lips down her body, pausing on her nipples. I carefully roll it between my teeth, careful not to hurt her but letting her feel the strange sensation.

Chloe inhales and moves her hand down her shorts, undoing the button and touching herself.

"No, no," I say, teasing her and pulling her hand out of her shorts and pinning it above her head. I do the same with her other hand. It would have been helpful to be at home where I have silk ties and handcuffs, but this will have to do for now.

"Please," she begs.

I take mercy on her and put my mouth between her legs, kissing her clit before I start to tongue her. She moans in delight as I continue to lick her.

I add a finger inside her and watch her face as I reach her G-spot.

"Oh my god," she moans. I silence her with a kiss.

I pull myself out of my shorts with my other hand and start slowly stroking, getting myself ready to take her.

I add pressure around myself and I start to swell even more. Chloe is dripping wet so I'm able to easily thrust into her.

She moans as I enter her and I have to pause for a moment to collect myself before I continue. She has no idea the power she has over me.

I look into her eyes and I can tell she's hungry for me. I thrust in and out of her harder, bringing her to her peak. The feeling of her walls tightening around me in an orgasm. The feeling brings me over the top myself, until we're both satisfied.

Chapter Eleven

Chloe

Dom leads me off the private beach and back toward the hotel. I'm a little uneasy on my feet after the way he made me feel on the beach.

I need to go back to my room and take a shower, I know there's sand in my hair - and plenty of other places - that it probably shouldn't be.

I try to smooth out my hair. I know it's wild from galavanting around the beach, but I want to look slightly less suspicious.

I know it's a rule not to play out in the open where people can see you, but I know that rule isn't always followed. I've seen it myself. And there are plenty of people like Dom who like watching.

"So what made you want to come here?" I ask.

"I was here once with someone I was seeing at the time," he says. I can tell he's holding back, he probably doesn't want to talk about exes with me.

"A girlfriend?" I ask.

"Not really, just someone I was seeing casually. We wanted to go on a vacation and we were interested in the lifestyle. It was easier because we weren't in a committed relationship. And that's when I discovered that voyeurism might be something that I was really interested in," he says.

"Have you ever been here with a girlfriend?" I ask. I want to know if he's been part of the lifestyle in a serious relationship. It's something I would like to engage with if Dom and I did commit to each other, but I know it's not always easy to see someone you're in love with playing with someone else.

"No, I haven't," he says.

"Any reason why?" I ask.

"I haven't done much in a serious relationship," he says, "to be honest, Chloe, I've never had a girlfriend before."

My mouth gapes open. I close it, trying not to embarrass him. There is no way he's reached his late twenties and never had a serious relationship. He's experienced with women, that's for sure. He's proven that much, he knows what he's doing. And he's just such a great guy, I can't imagine he has a hard time finding someone to be with. Being a company co-owner and a family man, he brings a lot to the table.

"I guess this is by choice?" I ask.

"Yeah, you could say that. I'm just busy, you know? I think my priorities are with work. Though it is something I've thought about more recently," Dom says and looks over to the ocean.

"Has anything changed?" I dare to ask, my chest exploding in butterflies as I suggest what we're both thinking.

"It has. A lot has changed recently. I see my sister with his kids, and they're just the best. The best times of the month are when I make my way home to visit. And there's just chaos, you know? She's making lunch in the kitchen, my brother-in-law is playing with the kids and the dog is barking at them, all excited to get involved. Anyway, it's great. And I realised I want that."

"Do you have the ability to not work?" I ask. I'm under no delusion that he needs to keep working, I know that Aegis is worth a lot.

"I don't want to give up my position, at least not yet. But I could take a step back and hire someone to work closer with me and eventually take over when I leave. Maybe in five or ten years we'll have built up enough that I can live off my investments. But I need to make sure it would be a comfortable living for me and...whoever I end up with," he says.

It sounds nice, Dom living on the farm and us having a couple of kids and lots of dogs running around. I can tend to the garden and work on fundraising so we can afford to take in more animals who need a place to live, and he can work remotely.

But he hasn't said it yet. It might not be me in that future he's imagining. And it would take years for us to reach that point, I don't know if either of us could do long distance for that long.

And I come with so much baggage with Justin. I don't know if he'll ever leave me alone.

I think he's just my problem to deal with. I don't want anyone else getting hurt.

Dom walks me back to my room. I'm I desperate need of a shower and some clean clothes. And maybe a glass of red wine, he's given me a lot to think about.

"Thank you for coming with me," he says, leaning in to kiss me.

"Thank you for… everything," I say and laugh.

"Are you still interested in the masquerade party tomorrow night?" He asks.

"I would love to. I have my mask and my dress all ready to go," I say.

"Amazing. I can't wait to see it."

"Meet me there? If you can't recognise me in the mask then maybe you weren't as interested in me as I thought you were," I say playfully.

"I promise you that will not be an issue," he says, "anyway, I'll leave you to it. Call me if you need anything."

"Oh and Dom," I say and he turns back around to me.

"If you want to play with anyone else at the party… it's fine," I say, "I know we're not serious at the moment. If you want to be with anyone else, it's fine. And you never know, it could be fun," I say.

"I think I can manage that. And if there's anyone you're interested in, it's fine. I'd love to be invited though," he smiles devilishly.

I'm sure he doesn't have to worry about not being invited.

Dom leaves to go back to his room.

I grab a quick shower and put on a clean pair of denim shorts and a loose-fitting T-shirt. I miss the comfy clothes I wear on the farm. Dressing up and laying in the sun is nice, but I think I'll always feel more comfortable in the overalls or shorts and a t-shirt.

I brush out my medium-length blonde hair, making sure I got all the bits of sand out. I think I'm going to stay in my room for the rest of the day and maybe order room service. I call Jas to check in with her and she picks up on the second ring.

"How's your vacation?" She asks.

"It's been good. Dom's been great," I say.

"I'm glad you're having a good time," she says, but her smile looks forced. I've been friends with her for long enough to know when something's wrong.

"What's up?" I ask, my face dropping.

"It's just Justin. He's been calling around and asking for you," she says.

"He has a no-contact order. He can't call around chasing me," I say.

"I know. And I told his probation officer, so she's aware. But there's not much they can do right now."

"They can lock him up for breaking probation."

"Yeah, but they didn't. They know you're out of the country right now so you're safe," she says.

"How did Dom know I wasn't at the farm? You said he called looking for me," I say.

"I was looking at the cameras. I saw him walking around outside. I called the police and called the farm hand and he was on high alert until the police got there," she says.

"What about the animals?" I ask.

"They're all fine," she says, "I've had the cameras on all day, just playing on my laptop. The police know about him and they know about the animals," she says, "please don't worry about them," she says.

"How am I not supposed to worry about them?" I ask, "I need to come home," I say.

"And what will you do when you're home?" Jas asks.

"Make sure the animals and the house are safe, obviously."

"There's nothing more you can do for them. The police are aware if I call them or if James calls then they come over straight away."

I like James and I don't want him to get hurt. He's always there for me if I need help with the animals or if I go away for a couple of days. He cares about the animals as much as I do, and I don't want him to be in danger.

"I don't know, Jas…"

"Chloe, please. You're safer there than you are here. Justin knows the police are on his ass, and if he comes around again he'll be arrested," Jas says.

"I guess so," I say.

"Do you have any plans with Dom? Or that woman you met, what was her name… Amelia?" Jas asks.

"I'm supposed to see Dom tomorrow night. There's a party," I say.

"I know those are very interesting parties," she laughs. Jas and her wife are not involved in the lifestyle at all, but she knows all about me and what I'm interested in.

"It should be fun," I say.

"Don't let Justin ruin your trip. You're safe there and everyone is fine. Have some fun, you deserve it," she says.

I nod and agree. I'm not letting him control my life any more, it's not about him.

It's about time I gave myself permission to life my own life on my own terms.

Chapter Twelve

Dom

It's finally time for the masquerade party. I'm nervous that Chloe and I won't recognise each other, but I get excited at the idea of the party.

Benji and Amelia won't be here tonight, I think he wanted to introduce her to the pain and pleasure room while most of the other guests are at the party. Which is fine by me, there will be playing out in the open and under no circumstances do I want to see Benji doing anything with anyone, and I don't want to be held back thinking he might see me. As long as our paths never cross, everything will be fine.

I choose my nicest black suit, the one that I reserve for black tie events and when I go to the occasional high-end lifestyle party. It's a deep, rich black in a luxurious fabric. It's custom so it's tailored to fit me exactly. I add a matching black shirt and a thin red tie. The trousers are also black, and my shoes are a shiny patent black leather with red soles, and I have matching red socks.

I smooth some gel through my hair, pushing it back and running my hair through it a couple of times. I spray a generous amount of Bleu de Chanel. Finally, satisfied with how I look, I put on my mask.

Yesterday the on site shop was taken over by masquerade masks. Some people brought their own if they knew about he party, which I didn't until Chloe invited me. I've been to them before while I've been here, but they're not hosted every week so I didn't think to check.

I don't have one at home anyway, but some people takes these events very seriously. Some even have masks adorned with expensive Italian lace or dotted with freshwater pearls or gemstones. It's expected to dress to impress. I chose a matte black mask that covers most of my face.

Satisfied with my appearance, I put my phone and wallet in my jacket pocket and left the room.

I see a number of other couples and individuals walking toward the bar as well. They normally have them inside but the parties are popular, so they'll often spill out onto the terrace, though playing is strictly inside to avoid any awkward encounters with other hotels in the area of any boats.

Chloe and I agree to go alone and meet there. There's something sexy about casual role-play. We meet each other in a dark lounge, and we're instantly taken by each other. Have our way with each other, still pretending to be anonymous and to never see each other again.

I've been imagining it all morning. Perhaps someone watching us have fun and joining in, or me watching Chloe with someone else or a couple.

As long as she still comes home with me, everything is fine. That's the best part, seeing other men lust after her but knowing that I have her to myself at the end of the day. Knowing that she is fully taken with me and she doesn't want to be with anyone else.

I arrive at the lounge and I'm greeted by a beautiful woman in a tight fitting dress who offers me a glass of champagne. She isn't one of the regular hotel employees, they're never involved in places or events where play might take place. They hire models and bartenders who specialise in lifestyle events. While they're strictly forbidden from participating, they're aware of the activities and sign an extensive NDA to ensure our anonymity.

I accept the glass of champagne as I enter the lounge.

It's still early in the evening, but there is a good turn out so far. I do a quick scan of the room and don't see anyone I recognise. Of course, that's more difficult because of the masks, but if I saw Benji or Amelia I would beeline out of there, but they're nowhere to be seen.

Chloe isn't here either and I wonder if she's changed her mind on coming. I hope she's just taking slightly longer to get ready.

I finish the glass of champagne and make my way up to the bar.

The model is beautiful, with a form-fitting pink satin dress and a light pink mask just covering her eyes. Her high cheekbones are still visible just under the mask.

"Hello, lovely," she says, "what can I get for you?"

"Can I have a whiskey on the rocks please," I ask.

"My pleasure," she says.

While she makes my drink I do another scan of the room for Chloe. I check my phone, but there are no messages from her. I quickly put it back in my pocket, I don't want to be seen with it out for too long.

Phones are highly frowned upon at lifestyle events. Some events will make you lock them up before any play, but Indulgence Island is a place that has earned a lot of trust over the years and caters to people who have been in the lifestyle for many years, so they know the rules here and wouldn't want to be banned from coming back. I like being able to keep my phone just in case there are any issues.

I know Chloe said I can be okay without her, but I want her to still be involved.

I still struggle with the fact that I'm falling for her. I can't do that, I'm way too busy. I need to make sure Aegis keeps growing strong. There's still so much we haven't done yet, and I can't get distracted.

But a man still has needs. And goddamn I need her.

I accept my glass from the bartender and glance once more at the door. I feel a deep exhale exit my chest as I see her.

Chloe.

She's wearing a burgundy dress that's form-fitting on the bodice but the skirt is beautifully full and pleated. I imagine sending my hand up the skirt and I feel myself harden at the idea. The warm lighting bounces off her collarbone which is gently outlined by the thin straps on her dress.

She's wearing a silver mask that covers most of the upper half of her face, but I would recognise that figure and golden blonde hair anywhere. She accepts a glass of champagne from a model walking around with a tray and scans the room.

"Hello, handsome," Chloe says.

"I thought you weren't supposed to recognise me," I say.

"I would recognise you anywhere," she says and pulls me in for a small kiss.

"So, what are your plans for tonight?" I ask.

"Well, I'm going to flirt with you a little. And then I'm going to… explore, maybe," she says, leaning in to close to me. God, she's killing me. She smells like roses and a slight tint of vanilla. Her lips are emphasised with a light pink lipstick, and she bites her lip slightly as she says it. She gently puts her hand on mine and her fingers creep up my sleeve slightly.

I want to take her home and rip her beautiful dress off. I want her to take my jacket and trousers off and throw them on the floor. Hell, she could burn the expensive suit if she wanted to, as long as we both had no clothes on, I didn't care how it happened.

But I know it would be much more satisfying if we dragged it out a little more. I wanted to watch her explore and be brought to the edge of orgasm. And then stop, because she didn't want anyone to take her there except me.

"How has your day been?" I ask and perch myself on a bar stool, and Chloe does the same. Her skirt rides up slightly as she sits down and I eye her tanned thigh, which doesn't help the problem I have developing in my boxers.

"It has been amazing," she says, "I checked in with the animals and they're all fine, thankfully. We have another adoption application for one of the dogs so I need to review that later. Jas already looked and she said the family was promising."

"That's amazing," I say.

"I would miss them for sure, but it's always so good when one of the dogs gets to go to a good home," she says, "and what else happened today… I went out kayaking with Amelia, that was pretty intense. I don't think I'll ever go kayaking again but we don't need to discuss that. Oh, and I met a friend. She should be here tonight, actually."

"What's her name?" I ask.

"Lizzie," she says, "and she is so *hot*."

"Is that right?" I ask.

I've had some suspicions but I didn't want to make any assumptions. But it was hard to miss the way that she looks at Amelia and the other women when they walk in to a room, and the way she enjoyed being with Ruby.

"Seriously, she is. And she's not here with anyone. I don't think she's met many people here yet. Oh, there she is," Chloe says and starts waving across the room.

"Hello," she says as she walks toward us.

"I think we should go without the introductions tonight… you know, the theme of the party and all," I motion toward the mask on my face.

"Bold of you to start making demands when we've only just met," she says and leans in to give me a hug. I quickly return the hug and give her a quick kiss on each cheek. I don't want Chloe to get the wrong idea that I'm more interested in her friend. Though if she wanted to play together, I wouldn't say no.

We talk and have a couple of more drinks. As the night moves on we start dancing and one of the other couples begins the play. A man and a woman I've never met are on the couch. Their masks are on and he hikes up her skirt and slides his hand up her thigh. She dramatically throws her head back and moans. I can tell she likes performing, and I'm happy to watch.

I lean into Chloe and give her a long kiss while keeping an arm wrapped around Lizzie.

Chloe pulls away from me and has a mischievous smile on her lips as she leans in and kisses her friend. It was going to be a long night, and we were just getting started.

Chapter Thirteen

Chloe

Lizzie is an old friend from the last time I was here. She comes to Indulgence Island a couple of times a year, so it's not uncommon for her to be here multiple weeks of the year. I don't exactly know how she can afford it. Something like her Dad owning a diamond mine. Or maybe an Emerald mine, I can't remember.

Either way, she doesn't have to work a traditional job. I follow her on social media, and if her feed is to be believed she spends most of her time travelling and reviewing restaurants and posting pictures of new outfits in beautiful places.

I think she comes here just to relax and take some of the pressure off.

I don't think it's a difficult life to be an heiress with a large social media following and spending time in beautiful places, but I think she's alone most of the time. I don't think she has many friends. Though she's beautiful so when she's here, she's very popular.

She has naturally tanned skin and long brunette hair. There's a slight highlight in her hair, but it looks natural from the sun. She spent some time walking runaways for a high-end lingerie brand and her figure is proof of that.

She must have seen my pictures on social media and recognised the resort because she messaged me a couple of hours before the party. She's going to land and just in time to meet up.

We've been together before, on a trip a couple of years ago.

She was fun, and I've been looking forward to meeting up ever since.

It's difficult to kiss with my mask on, but I make it work. Her lips taste the same as I remember. Slightly minty from gum, the slightly waxy texture from her lipstick, but still sweet and gentle.

She uses her lips to part mine and gently lick her tongue into my mouth. She puts her hand on the small of my back, pulling me in closely.

I want to open my eyes and see if Dom is looking at us, but I don't want him to know that I'm trying to impress him.

I very much want to be intimate with Lizzie again, she is incredible and I've been looking forward to this since the last time we were together.

I feel Dom's hand stroke across my shoulders. I think he's trying to break me away from Lizzie, so we operate and I look up at him. There's a wild hunger in his eyes. He wants me and that much is obvious. He leans in and kisses me before looking over at Lizzie and kissing her. I feel a heat spreading across my body, seeing the two of them together. Not the usual jealously one would expect, but excitement.

I know he doesn't have any feelings for her, and I think that is what makes it better. He might desire her, and even have sex with her. But he wants me to be the one to fall asleep with him and wake up with him at the end of the day.

And I know he would love to see Lizzie and me together. Who am I to deny him of that?

I take a look around the room. There are people still talking, drinking, and flirting, but plenty of people have started playing. I take a long drink of my champagne, finishing off the glass.

There's a man and a woman already wearing nothing but their masks while he sits on the couch and she sits on her knees, going down on him. He holds the back of her head, pushing her head further onto his large member.

"Looks like fun," Dom says, whispering into my ear.

"Do you want to get away from the bar?" I ask and Lizzie nods. Dom waves over one of the servers and takes three glasses of champagne off the tray, handing one out to each of us.

We make our way over toward the couches. There are three areas, each with three couches facing each other. I sit down on the black leather. It's lined in plastic, normal for when they expect group play. It's not the nicest to sit on but it works for me. Much better than playing on something gross.

Dom motions for us both to sit on the couches and I obey. I wonder what it's like for him to be dominant. So far I've seen him in more submissive roles while watching. But Dom has a very commanding presence. I think he would do well taking charge.

He positions himself between us, on his knees. It's strange to see him in a position like that but I trust his judgement.

He kisses up my leg and in between my thighs, spreading my legs apart and hiking up my dress. I can feel eyes on us. There are more people playing now. Most people wait until one couple get started and then take that as an invitation to either join in or start their own play. Dom slowly pulls my legs apart and I let him. I'm more exposed than I normally am, but I like it. I can feel people looking at me and desiring me. He teases my clit, making me drip with anticipation.

He looks up at me playfully before licking me.

I moan with delight and just as I'm enjoying it, he stops.

Dom moves toward Lizzie and does the same, but this time looking at me. I get hot while watching him enjoy her.

"Oh my god," she says and grinds her hips back and forth while he licks her.

He puts a finger inside her and I can't help but reach down and start to pleasure myself.

There's a couple across from us who have started playing as well. A man and a woman, I think they're married. I've seen them around the pool and the lounge bar and I've always seen them together. They're good-looking. Older than me but still attractive and fit.

Dom makes his way back over to me and I stop touching myself, letting him take over.

The man across from us locks eyes with Lizzie. She nods her head and he comes over, his wife watching and enjoying it.

He quickly reaches over and grabs a condom and pushes his way into Lizzie.

"I guess I'm not needed there any more," Dom says and laughs. I kiss him and pull him close to me. His mouth is wet from pleasuring both of us.

"Sorry," Dom says laughing and wipes his mouth.

"It's fine. I find it hot," I say.

"Is that right?" He says and puts his hand behind me, holding onto the top of the couch.

"I would love to see the two of you together," he says, "but for now, I've decided you're all mine."

He pushes himself into me and I moan.

"Oh my god. Is it bigger than normal?" I ask.

"I think I'm just very excited," he says, "that can happen sometimes."

He looks me in my eyes as he forces himself the rest of the way in, using the back of the couch for leverage.

"You look incredible," he says while thrusting into me.

"Everyone is looking at us," I say.

"Some people are playing, they're in their own little world. But yes, some people are," he says, pushing into me suddenly, making me jump. But I like the tidbits of domination he displays.

I can tell he's showing off a little as well, which I'm happy for him to do.

He plays his hand on my clit and starts rubbing. I can tell I've held back a little. While I've done plenty of swinging and small group sessions in the past, I've never done anything like this in a large room of people before. I can tell I'm holding back.

"Relax," Dom whispers in my ear, "you're so tense."

I close my eyes and lay my head back, feeling him thrusting into me and using his thumb to circle my clit.

He starts pumping faster and faster until I feel myself going over the edge.

My body shakes in a satisfying climax. I look over and Lizzie is still with the other man, but by now they've switched so she's sitting on his lap and bouncing up and down while his wife watches on, her hand up her skirt, playing with herself.

Dom pulls my head back over to focus on him, and he kisses me just before finishing and filling me up.

Chapter Fourteen

Dom

I spend the next morning nursing a killer hangover. I should have known champagne would do that to me.

I've been intentionally ignoring my phone. I don't want anything to do with work, or dealing with any family problems.

Chloe is still in my bed, her blonde hair a mess next to me. Some of the strands have ended up on my pillow as well. I was pushing it out of my face all night. I spent the entire night with her in my arms, not daring to let her go.

She impressed me so much yesterday. I could tell that being in public was something out of her comfort zone.

When we finally made it back to the room, she fell asleep almost immediately.

I don't know what happened after she went back to her room the other night after we had our little date on the beach, but I think something happened. She's been tense ever since. I want to contact her friend Jas and see if everything is ok at home, but I don't want to overstep.

I pull out my phone and see a flurry of messages. Most of them are from Marco, Benji's assistant.

Have you spoken to Benji yet today? He asks.

No, I send back

I need him to call me, he says.

He was planning on spending the night with Amelia, and it's still early. I'm sure he's still asleep.

What's going on? I ask.

I really need to talk to Benji he says.

Fuck sakes, Marco. You know I'm as involved in this as he is. I wish people at the office would stop diminishing what I do. I own the company just as much as Benji does. We have different job roles, but the company never would have expanded without me. Benji will acknowledge it, but no one else does.

I decide he is a lost cause and look at some of the other messages.

There's a text from my sister.

I'm almost afraid to ask, but where are you and Benji on vacation? Caroline says.

My heart starts racing. Why would she ask me that?

There's an email from someone on the PR team. She linked me to an article which I click on.

I briefly read the article. It's about exposing who actually goes to swingers resorts. What the hell?

I scroll back up and look at the author name.

Amelia Cooke.

That mother fucker.

There's a part of the article about how two people there are good friends who own a tech company. Could she have made it any more obvious if she tried?

I can't believe it. Did Chloe know about this?

There's nothing in the article that only Chloe would know. There's really not even much about me in particular, so that's good. I hope Chloe hasn't been an informant for her, but I need to know.

I look over at her, still sleeping. I can't wake her up yet and I don't want to interrogate her as soon as she wakes up. There's plenty of work to do until then, so I get started.

First, I get back to Caroline and lie to her, assuring her that's not us and that's not the resort we're staying at. We could be anywhere in Mexico, and I don't think she'll be checking my location to find the answer to something she doesn't really want to know. My sister is on a need-to-know basis about me living in the lifestyle. In that, she doesn't need to know anything.

I write out a quick email to the PR team outlining what we're doing. The first is contacting the publication to see if we can have the article revoked. So far some people are asking us on social media if this has anything to do with us. We're not trending and there aren't too many comments coming in about it. It's enough to scare me. We choose not to delete them, or that would look too suspicious.

As I'm finishing up fighting fires, Benji finally wakes up.

Did you see the article? He texts me.

I did. I've been on it, you're CC'd on all the emails with PR. They have a game plan. So far it looks bad, but not too bad. We should be fine. You need to talk to Marco, he was frantic this morning. I say.

Good. Seems like you've got it under control, he says.

Of course, I had to clean up your mess while you were sleeping. Meet me at the tennis court at 12? I need it. I need to hit something very hard to let my frustration out.

Sounds good. Then we can talk and come up with a game plan, he says.

I wonder if Amelia is still with him. That would be an interesting conversation.

Chloe wakes up half an hour later and I briefly explain to her there's an issue with work that I need to deal with, and then I'm going out with Benji to discuss it a bit more. She's fine with that and leaves to go back to her own room and give me some space.

I can't believe that last night was so incredible, and now we're dealing with this instead of enjoying the morning together.

I get ready and walk over to the tennis court, grabbing two rackets and a couple of tennis balls on the way over.

Thankfully I brought some gym wear. I wasn't confident I would actually work out here, knowing I would have a hangover most days.

"Good morning, Sunshine," Benji says as I storm into the tennis court.

"You've really fuck it up this time," I say.

"You think I had any part in approving this?" He asks.

"Have you spoken to her today?" I ask.

"Yes,| he says, serving the ball, "she regrets it. She came clean about everything. She didn't want to write the article. She was sent here with work to write it, she didn't expect to actually like it here. And you know, meet someone," he shrugs.

"You're entirely too casual about this," I say.

"It's fine. No one has really made the connection yet. I've kept an eye on social media and the buzz has died down. None of the investors know about this."

"Caroline asked if we were here," I say.

"And I'm assuming you denied it?" He asks.

"Obviously I wasn't going to tell my sister where we were."

"And she believed you, I'm sure. It's fine. Everyone will chalk it up to a weird coincidence," he says. I hit the ball as hard as I can and score a point.

"You're losing your touch," I say. We used to play a lot of sports in university whenever we could get away from classes or work.

"I was never that good," he says, "if I was good at sports and computers, while looking like this, I would have been too powerful."

Naturally, I demolish him in the game.

Benji and Amelia are on rocky terms but he still wants to make it work with her. I don't blame him, she does seem really nice, and I know he is slightly obsessed with her.

Amelia is going home in just a couple of days. Benji talks with he front desk staff and he's able to add her to his room and she can stay longer. I barely want to see her, but I'll tolerate her being here for Chloe and Benji's sake.

I catch up with Chloe later. She's not happy with Amelia, especially because Chloe was mentioned in the article. Though it was vague enough I don't think anyone would make the connection.

Amelia and Benji continue to work on getting the article revoked.

If it comes down to it, we can get Aegis' lawyers involved. But I really don't want to. I don't know what Amelia's employment plans are, but I'm sure that would not bode well for her. Knowing Benji, he's probably going to try to take care of her while she's still in school, but that's all up to her.

I try to put my feelings aside and focus on the rest of the trip. Marco and the other higher-ups at Aegis are working fine with it, and the projects are going well.

Maybe Benji was right, and we never should have left the office. This is by far the most stressed I've ever been while on a vacation.

Chapter Fifteen

Chloe

I haven't spoken to Amelia too much about the article. I know she feels bad about it, but I'm still angry about it. I don't need anyone in my real life to find out about it. I know Dom is fuming mad about it. I don't blame him, he really put him and Benji in a tricky situation. But from what I've gathered, the PR team at Aegis are managing it well.

I haven't told either Dom or Amelia about the text I received earlier that day.

Are you at Indulgence Island?

The sender was a phone number I didn't recognise. I have Justin blocked on everything, but he will always manage to contact me if he wants to. I took a screenshot of it for evidence and blocked the number straight away. But I know if he wants to, he'll manage to get a new one. He probably has burner phones at the ready just in case he wants to say something.

I decide not to tell Jas either. Keeping it to myself probably isn't the best, but I don't want to worry anyone.

I've been checking the security cameras constantly and messaging James. He assures me everything on the farm is fine and there's nothing wrong om the cameras.

I did send the screenshot of the message to my lawyer, who said she would look into the number and see if we can prove that Justin sent it. But until then, there's nothing else we can do.

We're leaving tomorrow, so I pack up and take my things over to Dom's room. I want to spend the last night here with him so I'll make sure I can leave straight from his room, and then the four of us are taking a taxi over to the airport in the morning.

I need to talk to him about where we're heading once we leave. I know he's not one for commitment, and I said I would never live with a man again, but I can't help but feel that I want to wake up with him every day.

I get my suitcases and double-check that I haven't left anything in the room, and I take the elevator upstairs to Dom's room. He's been expecting me so the door is propped open

"All ready to go?" Dom asks when he sees me in the doorway of his room.

"Unfortunately, yes," I say.

"I wish we could stay here forever," he says.

"Start working from home. We can split our time between here and the farm," I say, only half joking. I would like to visit more often but I wouldn't be able to leave the animals that much. And I think Dom would miss his family if he moved too far away from them.

Dom's suitcase is open on the bed and he's packing his things and I sit on the balcony reading my book.

As he finishes packing up, I motion Dom to come out to the balcony with me.

We look out over the balcony. The view is incredible, I feel like we should have been up here more. The waves crash against the sand on the beach as couples walk hand in hand. Just below us, I can see the pool surrounded by loungers, where individuals are reading or talking to friends. There's a group of women playing a game of cards at a table, and two men playing game of table tennis next to them. There are not too many people out as the dinner service has just started and the sun is starting to set over the horizon. The sky is painted with beautiful pink and orange streaks from behind the cliffs.

"It's so nice out, come look," I say as Dom finishes packing up.

"Wow, it's incredible out here," he says, "but not as beautiful as you."

He leans in and gives me a gentle kiss.

"That's so corny," I say, "has that line ever worked for you before?"

"I'm not sure. I've never used it before. Hopefully it works," he says.

We stand there for a moment watching the tide come in. I feel Dom's hand move across my ass and gently reach up my sundress.

"It's still daylight, someone might see us," I say.

"Lucky them," he says, his hand continuing up my skirt as he kisses my neck. I will admit, it feels nice for him to adore me.

His hands work their way up my skirt and find my underwear. I'm not wearing shorts under my skirt, it would be way too warm for that. His fingers cross my underwear, teasing me. I know he could have me now if he wants to, but he wants me to desire him. I already do, but he wants me to *need* him.

His fingers flick inside my underwear and I feel relief knowing soon he'll pleasure me.

When suddenly, he stops.

I look up at him, confused. Dom has a devilish grin on his face as he continues touching my wet underwear.

I finally feel him push my underwear to the side and his fingers easily glide inside me. A small breath escapes my lips as I feel the relief of his fingers circling my clit.

I can't make too much noise and risk drawing attention to myself.

Dom slowly positions himself behind me and unzips his shorts. I lean forward slightly and he pushes himself inside me.

"Good girl," he whispers in my ear, "you look incredible."

I have to bite my bottom lip to keep from making noise. We should be far enough away from people that they won't really notice what we're doing up here. There is a balcony on either side of ours so I don't want to make too much noise, though I don't think there's anyone out on their balconies.

I put my hands on the railing in front of me and arch my back as he pushes into me. I have to bite my lip from shouting out as I feel him enter me. I can feel so much more of him than I normally can, and he's already almost too much to handle.

He puts his hand on my hair and wraps it around my fist.

"You take it so well. Good girl," he whispers in my hair as he pulls my hair gently and continues thrusting inside me.

Dom removes his hand from my hair and puts it on my ass, squeezing me in his hand.

The sensation pushes me over the edges and shakes my body in an orgasm.

After a short time, Dom finishes too, quieting coming inside me while I try to act subtly.

We clean up and both get a shower. I'm tempted to go in and join him, but he needs to keep getting packed up, and if we keep seeing each other naked I don't think we'll ever be able to get ready to leave.

After Dom is packed up and the sun has set, we go out for one last date before leaving.

Dom's dark tan trousers and a button-down shirt, and I choose a blue and white maxi dress. Dom booked us a private dinner on the beach.

We make our way down to the beach which is just illuminated by the moon a candlelight. There's a bottle of champagne sitting in a chiller on the table.

"This is beautiful," I say. The waves crash against the beach but there are no other noises, we can't even hear the chatter of other guests or the music always playing in the lounge at night. Dom pours us each a glass of champagne as the appetisers are brought over to our table.

"Do you think you would move out of the city so we can be together?" I ask with bated breath.

"I would move to a different planet if you asked me to," he says.

"I'm a lot to handle," I say, "there are a lot of animals, and we're a packaged deal. And with Justin, I don't know when it'll all come to an end…"

"And I'll be there with you no matter what happens. I'll buy a pair of overalls and learn how to drive a tractor, or whatever you need. And then if anything does happen with Justin, I'm there for you," he says, reaching over the table to take my hand.

I feel a wave of relief wash over me. When we leave here tomorrow, we can make a plan to get him working remotely and moving to the farm.

Chapter Sixteen

Dom

I get home and drop my suitcases in the living room. I need to do my laundry, but I don't want to think about that now.

All I can think is that Chloe is gone.

We got on the same flight home together. It was nice, we shared snacks and watched movies. There was a comfortable silence on the way home, knowing that when the plane landed at JFK airport, I'd be taking a car with

Benji back into the city. Jas met Chloe at the airport in her truck.

It was nice to meet Jas, though it was a quick meeting outside the airport. She was kind, though I could tell she would tear me apart if I hurt her friend. But she brought Bruiser to greet Chloe. I thought he was going to knock her over with the joy of seeing her.

Returning home, my apartment feels colder than normal. The view of the skyline doesn't excite me like it should. I know there are thousands of people around me, but I don't care about a single one of them, because none of them are Chloe.

She keeps texting me during their long drive home. She hates Jas' country music, but she won't let Chloe change the radio station.

I would think a farmer would love country, I text her, smiling.

That is a reductive stereotype, she says, **I only like it when I'm line dancing**

I can't tell if she's serious or not.

I spend the next weeks at work in a daze. I live for FaceTime calls at the end of the day when Chloe is cooking dinner after finishing farm chores. I started taking a car home instead of the subway so I could get there as quickly as possible.

I start drinking more, but always at home. I haven't been out of the house in weeks unless it's to go to work.

Benji traps me in the break room during lunch one day. I've been eating at my desk to try to get my work done as quickly as possible so I can get home earlier. But I had to get a coffee and he had me trapped by the espresso machine.

"You need to go see her," he says.

"We have a big project due at the end of the month," I say, "I can't take any time off."

"Then pack up your laptop and go work from her place. I can't stand to see you like this any more. You have circles under your eyes, you look like shit, like you haven't slept in weeks."

"What about the meetings we have booked?" I ask.

"We live in the twenty-first century, Dominic. You can video call into the conference. Besides, you're not that important," he says, playfully punching my arm.

I know that's a blatant lie. But he's right about the distance working.

We have tried to be more flexible with other employees working. As long as it all gets done, I couldn't care less where in the world they were working from. Why wouldn't I do the same for myself?

I message Chloe when I get home from the office.

How would you feel about me moving with you? Feel free to say no, I don't want to move too fast. But it might be an option.

After she opens the message, I get a call come through.

"Are you serious?" She asks.

"Yes. Dom and I were talking about it. And all of my work really can be done from home. I'll just need to come into the city for conferences and the like. And I'll be in fairly often to visit Benji and Caroline, but yeah… I can pack up and leave any time," I say.

"What about your apartment?" Chloe asks.

"I'll give it to Caroline," I shrug, "the condo is paid off. She's living in an apartment the size of a shoebox and she has two roommates. She'll jump at a chance to have a place to herself. And might as well help her instead of selling it."

"Amazing. I can't wait. So when are you leaving?" She asks.

She and I agree that I'll rent a van and pack all my stuff up and move over the weekend. It's safer for her if I'm there anyway, and I can help with the farm chores. It'll be good for me to do some real work instead of just going to the gym.

I spend the next three days packing and arranging for the moving truck. I don't have too much here that I want to bring, just some clothes and personal items. I'm leaving the condo fully equipped for Caroline.

She was over the moon when I asked if she wanted the place. I gave her strict instructions to not destroy the place, sell everything I own, or host too many parties.

She's been getting to work closer to her start time and she's been participating more in meetings, so I have faith she might actually be turning her life around.

I leave as soon as I finish work on Friday. It's a long drive to Chloe's house, but I enjoy the drive there. I spent the night driving until I reached her late the next morning.

I turn onto a large estate. There's lots of space in front of the house, I can barely see it at the end of the long driveway. The gates are open, Chloe must have left them open last night, knowing I was coming. I wish she'd kept them closed last night, but she must just be excited that I'm finally getting here.

I pull up the long drive. The home is small, she must have prioritised the land the house edits on. It's a nice white home with dark green trim. There are flower bushes on the outside that are well-tended to.

As I pull up the driveway, the front door swings open and three dogs run out onto the front lawn, stopping short of the driveway. Chloe comes bounding out of the door just as I get the truck in park and get out. She jumps into my arms and I hold her tight. I lean her against the truck and kiss her.

"I missed you," she said.

"It's only been a couple of weeks. You couldn't have missed me that much," I say.

"I think I burned a battery out of my vibrator," she laughs.

I don't have a response to that besides the want to get her in bed immediately for a demonstration.

"Come take a look around the house," she says and takes my hand. Bruiser is wagging his tail so hard it looks like he might lose it entirely.

"Hey there Buddy, remember me?" I ask and offer my hand. He jumps up toward me.

"Bruiser, down. Sorry about that. They're trained not to run off the lawn, but he still jumps sometimes. He's harmless," Chloe says.

"No, it's fine. He's perfect," I say.

She shows me around the house. Jas isn't here and I wonder how far away she lives, but she must be close. Chloe uses the security system at the front door to close the gate and turn on the alarms.

"You'll get used to it. And I'll give you the key code in a minute," she says.

She shows me around the house. There's a bubbly sourdough starter on the counter, I have no idea how that works, but I'll have to figure it out so I can help her some time. There's a large greenhouse filled with tomatoes and strawberries.

"I'm working on preserving food so I can be more self-sufficient," she says, "there are a lot of tomatoes… hopefully enough for the year. We can freeze some, and use some for marinara sauce, ketchup, and salsa. It should be fun when they're all ripe and I need to make all of this in two days," she says.

She has dozens of books all about homesteading, canning, and farm animals. I make a mental note to start reading through them.

Her back garden is huge, taking care of it here must be a full-time job. Or hell, probably more than full-time hours.

All her furniture is older and worn, but it's sturdy.

"It's not fancy," she says.

"It's beautiful," I say.

"I was afraid you would be less than impressed. When Justin left, he took everything. I didn't have a lot, but I was lucky to get the house. So I had to refurnish everything myself. It took ages but I was able to source good items from thrift stores around the state."

She finishes giving the house tour and I unpack my items from the truck. I don't have to return it until tomorrow, and I don't want to leave anyway. I'm exhausted from driving all night but I don't want to spend our first day together sleeping.

We spend most of the day sitting on the back porch watching the dogs run around and having a beer until I retire for an early night. And for the first time in weeks, I sleep solidly because Chloe is in my arms.

Chapter Seventeen

Chloe

I'm running through a building, the fire alarm blaring. I'm in a long hallway with what looks like hundreds of doors on either side. I make a quick right turn and I'm in an identical hallway. It looks like an apartment building, but one I've never been to before. Why aren't I on the farm? Where is Dom? Why is the alarm so fucking loud?

I wake up when someone shakes me.

"Call the police," Dom says.

It takes me a moment to place myself. I'm at home, and Dom moved here yesterday to be with me. There's an alarm blaring. I look at my phone - 02:17. I press the side button quickly three times. After a few seconds, I'm patched through to a dispatcher. Dom has already grabbed the baseball bat I keep next to the bed and he's running downstairs in his boxers. Brusier is next to me, curled up at the bottom of my feet and looking up at my with concerned eyes. He doesn't know what the sound is and probably hates it. In between the alarm, I hear a commotion downstairs.

I try to throw on some clothes. There's a T-shirt and pair of sweatpants on my bedroom floor that I throw on over my palmas shirt and shorts.

It's nearly impossible to hear the dispatcher through the sound of the alarms. I yell my address and she says something back to me in a raised voice.

After struggling to hear for a minute, the alarms turn off and I'm left with silence.

"Can you hear me now?" The dispatcher says on the line.

"Yes. Did you get my address?" I ask.

"I did, and officers are on the way. They should be there soon, actually, your alarm company has already notified us. Is anyone else there with you?" She asks.

"Yes, my...boyfriend is here," I say.

"Is anyone hurt?" She asks.

"No," I say, "at least I don't think so. I don't know where my boyfriend is."

Dom must be downstairs trying to investigate. I open the blinds and look outside. There's nothing out there. I can see the front of my property line with floodlights in the distance, but it gets darker as I look closer to the house. I should have added more lights but we just have the motion sensor lights down there.

I'm frozen in place. I'm not sure if I should go investigate or stay where I am. But I can't hear anything downstairs. I need to check on Dom.

Bruiser is at my heels. He didn't move from me the entire time.

"Stay," I tell him, "you're better off in here."

I leave and close the door behind me with Bruiser inside. If anything happens and we need to leave, I'll come back for him.

I pad down the stairs, careful to look at the bottom of them before running out in to the hall.

The first thing I notice is that the front door is wide open. Two police cars with screaming sirens come racing up my driveway, flooding the house with blue and red lights.

These noises are awful, the animals are going to have a horrible time tomorrow.

I turn toward the living room and see it's a mess. My glass lamp is all over the floor, shattered. There's a large crack in the middle of my wooden table, with a spatter of blood on the living room rug.

"Hello, Chloe," one of the officers says. I can't remember her name, but she's always been nice. She has responded before when Justin has had an issue.

"My boyfriend should be here somewhere..." I say.

"We need to clear the area. Please stay here. Officer White will clear the upstairs while I look down here. We just need to make sure you're safe, that's all," she says. I sit down, feeling helpless. Dom is out there somewhere and I need to find him.

A couple of minutes later, Officer White comes back downstairs.

"The upstairs is clear, no one there," he says. I suspected that. I know Dom ran downstairs and it looks like all the action was down here, but at least no one was lurking in the spare bedroom waiting for me to wake up.

"Stay here, please," the officer says and the two of them go out to the front.

I want to call Dom and see if he can get the call on his smartwatch or his phone, but if he's hiding I don't want to give his location away.

Once the officers are outside, I take it upon myself to check the backyard. They can't be here all night, and realistically we know who it was. I've handled Justin by myself before and I'll do it again.

I open the living room closet and find the safe I had installed when I kicked Justin out last year. I enter the code and pull out the handgun I've had stashed in there. I never use it except once every other month when I go to the gun range to practice. I was hoping that I was being overly cautious by getting it, but I knew I needed something to protect myself.

I shrug on my large denim jacket and check the gun. The safety is on and there's ammunition inside. I place the gun in the deep pocket of the jacket and my phone in the other. I slip on some shoes and step out into the night.

I have to move fast. If either of those two cops find me, I'm going to be in trouble for leaving.

I take out my phone to use as a flashlight, but pretty soon I hear a crash from inside the barn.

I start jogging over and throw the door open.

"Justin!" I scream, "I'm going to fucking kill you, I swear to God!"

I pull the light switch and see Dom and Justin mid-fight. Justin looks over at me and Dom takes the opportunity to punch him in the face, slamming his body to the ground. Dom kneels on top of him and I quickly grab one of the ropes we use for the horses. It'll be tricky, but I try to tie his hands behind his back. I proceed to sit on his middle back so Dom can call the police again.

"Thanks for distracting him," Dom says.

"I felt like you needed my help," I say, "are you hurt?"

"I got a good whack to the head, but it's not too bad," he says.

I move to take a better look. I feel Justin's weight shift under me and I move my hand on his head to press him into the ground. He groans in pain and I lift my hand up. I don't want to hurt him too badly, I want to see him rot in prison. But I need him to know he doesn't have the upper hand any more. And he won't have it ever again.

The police officers enter the barn and I get up. Justin has given up, he doesn't try to get away when they put the cuffs around his wrist and pull him to his feet. I hear them read him his rights as Officer White takes him away.

The kind female officer stays behind for a moment.

"Well done," she says, "I don't love that you went out to find I'm yourself, you could have gotten hurt. But you're a strong woman. Well done," she says and gives me a small smile.

"Thank you," I say.

Dom puts his arm around me and gives me a gentle kiss on the top of my head.

"Let me see your wound," I say. He bows his head for me to take a look. It's small, but headwinds bleed a lot so there's a lot crusted into his hair. But it looks like the bleeding has stopped, which helps.

Dom and I check on the animals. The horses are spooked from the commotion, but they look fine.

The chickens haven't even noticed anything different, they're all still inside their coop. The dogs' shelter is soundproof, I knew it would be important around holidays to help keep out fireworks noise as much as possible. Some of them are awake and confused as to why they're being woken at such an early hour, but they're fine.

I look at my phone. It's just past three in the morning. My nervous system is still fully awake and my heart is just beginning to return to a normal pace.

We get back inside and check all the doors and windows and re-alarm the house and I return the gun to it's safe. I hope I won't have to think about pulling it out ever again.

Dom takes a shower to wash the blood out of his hair. While he does, I pour us two strong drinks.

Once he's done, we sit on the couch and have a couple of measures of scotch on the rocks. I don't feel like I can go back to bed yet. But as long as I'm here with Dom, I think I can face whatever's next.

Chapter Eighteen

Dom

I feel jumpy and uncertain the next day. Chloe and I woke up late after missing so much sleep. We had a couple of more drinks than we probably should have, but I needed it to calm down.

I was ready to kill Justin if I had to.

He's in lockup now where he spent the night. One of the police officers called us this morning and said that he wasn't going to get bail. The courts have finally had enough of his shit and they're keeping him until sentencing.

He's being charged with breaking and entering, assault, trespassing, and breaking his probation conditions. So he has to wait in the local jail until his sentencing.

"Do you think you're going to go to his court date?" I ask Chloe. She's been quiet this morning. I can only imagine what a toll last night was on her. She was a complete badass, but it's hard for your body to be in fight-or-flight mode for too long.

I pour her a cup of herbal tea instead of a coffee this morning. I don't think her nervous system needs the extra caffeine.

"I think I have to," she says.

"Don't you have a choice? If you don't want to you can send a victim impact statement or something to be read out," I say.

"I think I need to go. For closure. I want him to look me in the eye and know he never had a chance. I want never going to get back with him, and he was never going to hurt me again," she says.

There's a moment of silence before she speaks again.

"How do you think he got in?" She asks, "was it my fault for leaving the gate open for you?" She asks.

"No. Of course it wasn't your fault," I say.

"I bet he got in when I left the gate open," she says, "and then he broke the window to get in."

She might be right. Who knows how long he's been stalking the place out, and he saw the open gate and took the chance while he had it.

There's a black trash bag over the window. I added that last night to make sure no debris got inside the house. With Justin in custody, we didn't worry about anyone else coming in, we just couldn't let the living room get destroyed by the open window. There's a repair person coming in the afternoon to clean up the glass and replace the window.

"It's fine, please don't worry about it," I say, "there's nothing to worry about now."

He's locked away, and hopefully for a long time. Only time will tell, but I'll be here if he tries anything again. I just want to live our lives in peace.

I can tell the events of last night are taking a toll on Chloe. She's tired and lethargic, and not at all her bubbly self. She's moved out of the bed and underneath a throw blanket on the couch where she's nursing the morning coffee I brought her. It's not at all the way I imagined our first morning together. From the many phone calls we had in the mornings, I knew she normally woke up early to start the farm chores.

"Is there anything I can help you with this morning?" I ask.

Chloe is staring at the wall, as if in a daze.

"Oh," she says, processing what I've said, "yeah, the chickens need to have their eggs collected. And to be fed. Their grain is in the little shed."

"I'll do it," I say.

I'm taking the day off work. After the events of last night, I texted Benji and said I wouldn't be logging on today. Police might come by if they have any questions or need anything from us. And I don't want to take my focus away from Chloe at all.

I put on my pair of hiking boots I got for farm chores. And go outside to find the chicken feed. The air is crisp and cool as it's still fairly early in the morning. I seen the small shed next to the house. The door is unlocked so I'm able to get in and get the large bag out. I have a basket which I also need to use for the eggs, so I fill it with grain. I feel like Little Red Riding Hood taking the basket of food to her grandmother's house.

I open the coop and chickens start flocking toward me. I don't know how many there are. It's a huge coop, there could be a hundred of these guys in here waiting to pounce on me when I least expect it.

Immediately they start clucking at my feet. I'm surrounded but them and I'm afraid if I move a muscle I might step on one of them. I start sprinkling the food at my feet, making myself even more of a target than I was before.

I yelp as one of them pecks my lower legs. I thought the jeans would help protect me, but it doesn't feel like they're helping much.

I haphazardly throw some of the grain to distract the chickens and they start clucking in the other direction of me, leaving me alone.

How much do I feed them? I throw another handful in another part of the pen. I'm afraid they won't all eat if the food is all in one spot.

I remember Chloe telling me something about letting them run around in the yard every day, but I decide against it. I feel like I would absolutely lose one, or all of them.

I take the wicker basket and venture further into the chicken coop to collect the eggs.

How do I get it away from the chicken? I'm assuming there are no roosters in here, so I don't really know which, if any, are fertilised. Hopefully none of them are.

One of the chickens move and I quickly snatch the egg from underneath it. It doesn't mind, so I keep doing that. It's like whack a mole but it's with stealing eggs.

I decide to brave it and I pick up one of the ones sitting on an egg. It spreads its wings and I think it's going to kill me, so I drop it and flee the coop.

Chloe is standing outside looking at me like I have two heads.

"Sorry, I shouldn't have let you out here without a tutorial. I have a camera on the inside of the coop and it looked like you were struggling a little," she says.

"Yeah, you could say that I think," I say.

"You can get them out of here," Chloe says and lifts a small flap on the side of the chicken coop. She collects three of the eggs and lays them gently in the basket.

"That would have been good to know," I say. Chloe lets out a small laugh.

I know it'll take a while for her to feel like herself again. It might not happen until after Justin's sentencing, and even after she might still be impacted by the result. But I'll be here to make a fool of myself if that helps her.

Chapter Nineteen

Chloe

My lawyer calls us a week later. Justin has a date for sentencing. He's pleading guilty to the charges, but I'm still invited to come in and speak to the judge to make a statement.

The call rattles me. I've finally started feeling more like myself again, but I realise that I'm going to have to write a statement.

I've known that this is a possibility. And Justin pleading guilty is much better than him pleading not guilty and us having to go through a full trial. But in the back of my mind, I knew I was most likely going to have to write a statement about it, and I didn't know where to start.

I decide to take a break from thinking about it and I bring Dom another coffee.

Before he got here, I built him a desk in the spare bedroom so he could use it as an office.

Justin really picked a bad week to fuck up our lives. Dom's team is finishing the marketing for the new tech they're launching at the beginning of next week. He narrowly avoided having to go back into the office. We knew he'd be driving back and forth from the city and staying in hotels when he needed to, but we didn't expect it to be this soon. But Benji told him to stay around to help take care of me, which has been helping.

I've been starting to feel more and more like I can be a normal person again.

Dom logs off and closes his laptop.

"So what are we doing now that work is over?" He asks

"I was just going to read or watch TV," I say and shrug.

"No chance," he says, "we're going outside. It's lovely out there.

He's right. The weather is perfect for jeans and a light sweater, but the sun has gone down slightly so it's not too hot. It's the very beginning of early autumn, and it looks beautiful out there.

"I'm thinking we get a couple of the dogs and take them out," he says.

James has still been helping on the farm. I know I've been dropping the ball in that regard. But at least he still had the time to help me out, so the animals weren't suffering. But Dom is right, I should be trying to get out more.

I take the handful of leashes and Bruiser starts wiggling at the back door.

"Are we going to get your buddies?" I ask him and he starts howling I hand Dom half of the leashes and we make our way out to the dog kennels.

After clipping everyone on, we start walking down the path.

"It's handy to have a second person to help with this," I say as the dogs walk in front of me. Depending on how many dogs we have at any given time, I normally have to walk them in at least two or three groups. I often let them run around in the yarn off-leash a couple at a time, but it's nice to have them off the property a couple of times a week.

"It's beautiful out here," Dom says as we leave the fenced-in area of the back lawn and start walking through the woods.

"I thought I would be safer out in the middle of nowhere," I say, "but I think in the end it created more problems than I thought it would."

"He's behind bars. He can't hurt you now," Dom says.

"I know. I shouldn't be afraid, but I am. I guess my body isn't used to it yet."

I try not to get distracted by Dom struggling to hold the dogs. He has leashes in both hands and the dogs are getting tangled in each other.

"How do you do that so easily?" He asks. I have the leashes in one hand and I'm casually walking, the dogs all fine next to me.

"Lots of practice. And they're used to me," I say.

"So I only need a couple of years of practice? Sounds fine to me," he says.

After a while, we return back home. I felt like I needed the fresh air and the movement to be able to think. We have court in a couple of days and I need to write my statement.

* * *

It's finally court day and I'm freaking out a little. I've had nothing but trouble on deciding what to wear. I haven't eaten breakfast because I feel like I'm going to be sick. I have had a lot of coffee though to make up for the fact that I didn't sleep last night.

"You look nice," Dom says and gives me a kiss on the cheek. I settled on a navy blue dress. It's form-fitting but not too much so.

The pencil skirt hits me just below the knee. I add a black jacket over the top and a pair of black leather flats. My hair is smooth and flat ironed and my makeup is minimal. I didn't know if I would cry, so I made sure to add waterproof makeup.

"Thank you," I say and leave the front door. Dom is driving us in his truck so I don't need to worry about driving. There's a country station on the radio, the one he told me he was listening to when he first got here.

Dom hasn't left since he got here. Jas has delivered groceries and Dom hasn't returned to the city for work. I feel like I'm completely disrupting his life, but he hasn't complained about it yet.

It's a long and silent drive to the courthouse. My lawyer meets us outside the building.

"He'll be here, but he'll be on the opposite side of the room. He'll be handcuffed and in the prison uniform. I just like to warn people before they see the offender, it can sometimes bring up emotions," she says. I nod.

"Do you have your statement?" She asks.

"Yes," I say and pat the folded piece of paper in my tote bag.

"Good. You don't have to do it, but you've come all this way, I just want you to say your piece while you have the chance and then we never have to think about this ever again. Ok?" She asks.

I can do it. I feel my mouth go dry and my legs start to shake. I've never been good at speaking in public. Though this trial isn't a big event, it still makes me feel like my body is going into fight or flight mode. I know what to expect. There's no jury and it's not a big trial so there won't be an audience. Just a couple of other people in the waiting room and then inside it will just be the judge, Justin and our lawyers. I can do this.

I walk up the steps to the large brick building. After a couple of minutes, a woman calls my name and ushers me into the room.

It's a local courthouse, used mostly for domestic incidents and custody decisions, so it's small, unlike the grand ones I've seen in the movies.

The judge sits above us on a bench. A few moments later, Justin is guided into the room. I try not to look at him, but I can't help it. He looks like he's aged ten years and he's visibly lost weight. His hair is long and stringy.

He looks like a completely different person than the one I knew.

And to be honest, he looks pathetic.

When it's my turn to speak I stand up and direct the judge. I don't want to speak to Justin, but I want him to hear the way he's made me suffer.

I clear my throat before beginning.

"Your honour. Thank you for allowing me to take the time to speak to you today. Marrying Justin was a mistake that I will be paying for for the rest of my life. Before meeting him, I was innocent as to the ways that people can hurt you. I thought that when people made promises, they would keep them forever. Just in promised to be faithful to me, to be trustworthy, to protect me, and never hurt me. As soon as we were married he isolated me from my family and friends and broke every single promise he made to me. Throughout the past months after I separated from him, he made my life hell every day. He made me feel unsafe in my own home. He made me fear for the lives of my animals. I find it hard to trust people now. Even when he knew he was hurting me he didn't care. If anything, he wanted to see me suffer. I did nothing but love him and when I stood up for myself, I was punished for that. I just want him to be away so I can sleep at night again and I know that myself and other women won't be at risk any more. Thank you," I say and sit down. Dom quickly puts his hand on my knee to comfort me.

The attention turns to Justin quickly as he pleads guilty to the charges of assault, breaking and entering, and harassment.

The judge thanks us and we get up to leave. Justin's sentencing won't be for another week. I can make it that long, and at least he's behind bars in the meantime.

"Good job. You did well today," My lawyer says before getting in her car. Dom and I quietly get in his truck.

"How are you feeling?" He asks.

"Good," I say, "thank you for being here. I thought it would be harder than it was, but it was fine in the end. It's done now anyway. All we have to do is wait."

Dom reaches over and takes my hand, squeezing it slightly.

"You're incredible. I love you," he says.

Chapter Twenty

Dom

A couple of weeks later, we get a call from Chloe's lawyer. After court, she declined to come to see Justin's sentencing. She could have, but she said there was no need. She wasn't going to speak to the judge, and his decision is final. She said she didn't know what her reaction would be so she thought it was best to be at home for it.

She answers the call and puts her on speaker.

"Hi, I'm here with Dom," she says. I mute the TV and lean into the phone which she places on the coffee table. I've just finished work for the day so we were picking out a movie to watch while we have dinner. It must be one of her last calls of the day.

"Hi, Chloe, I hope you're OK. Forgive me for making this a quick conversation, but I need to get going. I've had a call from the court and Justin's sentencing has been decided," she says.

"Yes, I thought it might have been," she says.

"So the sentencing is done. He's sentenced to fifteen years before the possibility of parole. I'm sorry he has the chance of parole, but that will depend on his behaviour in prison. But he has time," she says.

Chloe is staring at the phone and I hear her exhale a long breath.

"Are you ok?" I ask and start gently rubbing her back.

"Yeah, I'm ok," she says, "I'm just glad it's over."

Chloe thanks her and ends the call. I can see she's tearing up.

"Chloe…" I don't know what to say. I want him to be behind bars for the rest of his life, but I don't even know if that's possible.

"This is incredible. Better than I ever could have imagined," she says.

"You're not upset he didn't get more time?" I ask quietly. It's hard to read her emotions.

"I'm ecstatic," she says, "we don't have to worry about him for another fifteen years. We can actually live our lives." A single tear falls from her eyes and she wraps her arms around me excitedly.

After a long embrace, I go into her small wine fridge and take out the bottle of champagne I was keeping for a special occasion. I was hoping it would be for good news like this, but if not it was going to be for when I give Chloe the ring I'm hiding in my sock drawer. Now isn't the time for that, I'm celebrating her and how much she's gone through to get to this point.

I pop the bottle and pour two glasses and bring one to her.

"You know, my alcohol consumption has gone up significantly since I met you," she says.

"It's not my fault that we're always celebrating. I would consider that a good thing, actually," I say.

"You know, you might be right," I say and reach over to scratch Brusier as he jumps up on the couch next to me.

Epilogue
Chloe
Four years later

Dom finally turns off his work laptop, just as I finish making dinner. He's holding down the fort at work while Benji is travelling. He and Amelia should be here any minute. I turn the oven down to warming and take the bottle of wine out of the fridge. I pour Dom a large glass and pour myself a sparkling water. Just as I do, I feel a hard kick in my belly, reminding me why I can't have a glass of wine with Dom. I've been missing it, but we wanted this pregnancy so badly that I don't feel bad about missing out.

Dom has been juggling parenting Sophie as well as working for the past half hour. I appreciate him looking after her while I'm in the kitchen.

"Mommy!" I hear Sophie shout and come barreling down the stair.

"Hi, Sweetheart," I say and wipe my hands on my apron before giving her a hug.

"I was helping Daddy with work," she says.

"Were you helping or were you distracting?" I ask.

"I was helping," she says and reaches up to the counter to take a fresh bread roll out of the basket.

"Thank you for taking here so I could get dinner ready," I say.

"It's fine, she attended the meeting with us. I think the investors have to say yes now, they completely fell in love with her," Dom says.

Aegis is opening another headquarters, the time in Chicago. They're finishing the last deals within the next couple of days.

The doorbell rings and Sophie runs to open it.

"Uncle Benji! Auntie Millie!" She squeals when she sees them on the doorstep. Amelia picks her up and gives her a big hug, as Benji pulls Dom in for a quick hug.

"Was your flight good?" Dom asks.

"It was great. I'm still getting used to first class," Amelia says.

"Come see my Mommy, she's pregnant with my little brother," Sophie says and takes Amelia by the hand and bring her in to the house.

"Hi, I wanted to give you a chance to get in the house before saying hi," I say and reach out to give her a hug.

"Look at that bump!" Amelia says while placing her hand on my belly. I only have another eight weeks to go before baby will be here so we decided on one final get together before Dom goes on paternity leave.

Benji and Amelia visit us at the farm a couple of times a year. It was difficult for the boys to get used to Dom not living in the city, but he loves it out here now. He loves walking the dogs on the weekends, and gathering the eggs in the morning with Sophie. And when he turns off his laptop at the end of the work day, he doesn't have to think about it any more. All he focuses on is our little family.

And I love having him here to protect us.

Camilla Harlowe is a thirty-something woman living in Kent, England with her husband and her calico cat.

She has been reading romance for years and is very grateful you have decided to give her a chance.

If you enjoyed the book, please leave a review on any platform you use. It means the world to indie authors.

Please follow her social media for book-related updates @camillaharlowe on all platforms.

Camilla has so much in store and she cannot wait to share these stories with the world.

If you've made it this far, thank you again for helping my dreams come true.

For updates and to shop please visit www.camillaharlowe.com

Or email camillaharlowewrites@gmail.com

Trigger Warning

Please enjoy this exclusive sneak peek at my next novel, 24601

24601 is a dark retelling of Victor Hugo's *Les Miserables*. A number of creative liberties have been taken to make this story my own. 24601 contains dark themes and is not suitable for anyone under the age of 18. Please be aware of the following triggers before reading.
- Corrupt police
- Suicide
- Child abuse
- Murder
- Conspiracy to commit murder
- Kidnapping
- False imprisonment
- Torture
- Dubious consent
- Blood play
- Knife play
- Mention of drug use
- Choking
- Gun use
- Drowning

Chapter One

Valjean
Present day

I stand in line while the idiot guard tries to count us for the third time. I'm not sure what the requirements are for being a guard, but they can't involve knowing second-grade math, because these fuckers can't even count.

The whistle finally blows and I can break my place in line and return to my cell. I start making a cup of coffee.

"Big day soon," my cellmate, Diaz says.

"Yep," I say, not wanting to engage. I pour a little more instant coffee into my cup than usual. I can tell he's going to be a pain in my ass again today.

It's true, I am getting out soon. But they don't tell us the exact date of our release. It causes too many issues with the other inmates. Rikers Island has too many lifers who have pent-up anger at themselves and the system. And after you've already killed once and you've gotten locked up for life, there's not many reasons not to do it again if even just to fuck with someone else.

But in the nineteen years I've been a slave in this prison, I've earned some respect here.

First and most importantly, my crime.

I could have gotten life. Some people argued that I deserved it. But some, and even the majority, thought I didn't deserve a day in jail.

I did kill. And I would again if necessary.

I caught my brother molesting my niece, Cosette. I walked in on him, his disgusting hands inside her pyjamas. The life was completely drained from her face. She was alive but dissociating.

My biggest regret was that she was still in the room when I strangled him with my bare hands. I happily watched the life drain from his eyes. When his eyes were bulging from his head and his body went limp, Cosette started crying.

I realised what I had done and picked her up and brought her downstairs. First I called her mother to come pick her up. I know my sister-in-law didn't want my brother alone with her. I know her treated his ex-wife like shit, but she managed to get out while she was pregnant. But for the past four years, he has been having her on the weekends. Over the past year though I'd noticed some strange behaviour in Cosette. She was afraid of her father. She had bruises and she wouldn't explain where she got them.

I expected something was going on. My brother was always a bastard, but I didn't expect this.

After I called her mother to come and get her away from this house of horrors, she called the police.

I tried to run, but that fucker Javier found me. And nearly killed me during the arrest.

I pled guilty and took an agreement of twenty years. I didn't want Cosette to go to trial as a witness. I just hoped that she was getting the help she needed and was maybe young enough to forget most of it.

After county jail, I got sent to Rikers Island.

When I first arrived, people gave me a little grief. After all, I'd never been in prison before. Sure, I did some things that should have wound me up in prison. But when I run I normally can't be found.

But of course, my name was all over the news.

The only people who had a problem with me were paedophiles themselves. And I didn't want or need any respect from them.

All the other guys in here would have done the same if they were in my shoes, so they mostly left me alone.

But nineteen years of living in a hole with a rotating supply of idiots as a cellmate is enough to drive anyone to insanity.

Nineteen years without a single visit. Not one update about Cosette, who has now grown into a young woman that I wouldn't recognise if she passed me on the street.

I have had hundreds of letters. They're all from strangers. Women with weird prisoner fetishes, or some people who are survivors of people like my brother. I did read every letter, in case any of them had any updates about Cosette. But they didn't.

I just hope she's still alive out there.

My brother took her innocence when she was alive. I won't let his memory take her life.

I finish my coffee and start washing the cup in the sink. It's Sunday, the one day every week I don't have work.

I've been working in the prison sweatshop for the past ten years. Only making enough money to buy coffee and a couple of soups each week.

I busy myself in my cell until it's time for me to go to chapel.

Besides the concrete walls, it's the most consistent thing I've had since I've been in here.

"24601," the guard shouts and I stand at attention. I turn around and put my hands through the slot in the door. Used for food trays when we're on lockdown, or more often for transporting from one area of the prison to another. He slides the cuffs around my wrist and they lock down, trapping me with the cold metal.

I hate these. The first time I was in cuffs I had a panic attack from the claustrophobia.

The thought that someone could come for me and I would have no way to defend myself.

Over the years, I have become more used to them. Thankfully I don't have to wear ankle shackles within the prison any more. One of the few perks of being on good behaviour while I've been here. But being in a maximum security prison for dangerous criminals, we have to keep the cuffs on.

I shuffle down the long hall and through a cage at the end of the hall. The chapel was an add on a couple of decades ago, so we get a brief moment of fresh air while remaining in the cage.

I enter the familiar building. A small chapel with few windows at the top of the building. No stained glass or any imagery on the walls. It's a multi-faith chapel, so it has to be used for everyone.

But today we have the priest. There is no service, just drop in one by one if requested.

"Valjean," the priest greets me when he sees me. He's been here even longer than I have.

"Hello, Father," I say and sit down at the pew at the front of the chapel.

"I hear your date is coming up soon," he says.

"It is. It's been a long time coming," I say.

"It's been well deserved," he says.

The employees and volunteers aren't supposed to research us, but I have a feeling he knows why I'm here. We've talked about it before - and I'm grateful he's one of the good ones. He has acknowledged that his peers don't always have the best track record with how they treat children. But he has not so subtly indicated he's on my side.

"Do you have any plans for when you get out?" He asks.

"I don't think you would approve of them," I say.

"Try me. We've known each other nearly two decades," he says.

He's right. Personally, if I was approaching eighty I would not be volunteering to spend my valuable last days inside a concrete block trying to get murderers into heaven. But that is the difference between him and I.

"A drink. And finding comfort in someone's bed," I say. I choose to leave out any illegal activity so as not to put him in an awkward position. Plus, there is a guard behind me.

"Do you have any plans for after your release that may lead you to be a productive member of society?" He asks.

I think about it for a moment. No, not really. Sure I've done the basics. I finished my GED since being here. I read more than I ever would have on the outside. But at the end of the day, I have no skills. No home. No family. Nothing to live for and nothing to do.

"You sound like my probation officer," I say.

The priest laughs. "I'm sure you're getting that question a lot at the moment. I won't press you too hard."

I hate my probation officer. She's an idiot, a little blonde girl who has never been locked up in her life. She keeps wanting me to have some connection or support to the outside. But I don't know how many times I need to tell her I don't have anyone. I know when I get out I'll be in a shelter or on the streets, running dope, the only way I know how to make money.

"What would you do? If you were in my position," I ask the priest.

He sits back and thinks about it for a moment.

"I know I would keep going to church. If nothing else for a warm place to stay and a warm meal after the service. But you need community, Valjean. You need someone you can rely on. Maybe you can find it there," he says.

"And what, find a nice wife and settle down with a home and have a couple of children? Work as an accountant?" I ask.

"You could do anything you set your mind to," he says.

"You sound like a school counsellor," I say.

"I think you could have used a school counsellor to guide you early on and we might not be in this situation," he says.

He knows I didn't like the therapist here either. I did my required sessions, but not a single one more.

"They didn't understand," I say.

"No, but you need someone to talk to. And I won't be here every week," he says.

"I've gotten better," I say.

"How have you been sleeping?" He asks.

"Better," I say. It's true, my sleep has been better. I'm up to a full four hours a night.

"It's going to be difficult to sleep in the shelter," he says.

It's hard to sleep when you have flashbacks every night in your dreams. As soon as I close my eyes, it sets me back. My little brother and I crying in our beds while our mother brings another random man in to have his way with her.

And they were never normal men. Always depraved, horrible people. Some tried their way with us, but that was the only time she put her foot down. She would always let them do what they wanted with her. Smack her around, call her degrading names. I figured that even if she said no they would have done it anyway.

Eventually child protective services found out and we were sent to live with our father. He was happy to have us there, so he could use us in his schemes. Children were a good distraction. No one thought the little kid was stealing your watch, but we got very good at that. If we refused, there was hell to pay. I was older than my brother Gabriel so I protected him as much as I could. But I could only do so much.

I did what I could to distract him. We would walk down to the library and check comic books out for him to read when he's up at night. Stories of superheroes that come and save you when you need it. I stole a tape player and headphones to keep him from the sounds.

But it didn't seem to work. He still turned into a monster, and it was my job to get rid of him.

Printed in Great Britain
by Amazon